BLACK OPS

SAMMIE D.

BLACK OPS

COPYRIGHT © 2016 BY SAMMIE D.

OPYTON PUBLISHING, RALEIGH, NC 27603

WWW.OPYTON.COM

ISBN (PRINT) 978-1-68225-006-8

ISBN (EBOOK) 978-1-68225-007-5

Chapter One

Vice President Aaron Woods sat behind his new desk in awe. This was his first official week in the office after being sworn in. The first meeting on his schedule was with Ryan Connors, his right hand man. Ryan appeared in the doorway with a light knock—right on time as always. He was carrying several files marked 'Classified'. Ryan wasted no time in getting down to business.

"Mr. Vice President, it is a privilege to be at your service. As you've been told, everything in these files is for your eyes only. Anything at this level does not exist outside of this office. That way, President Becker can't be held accountable."

"Yes, I understand. The orders are mine alone."

"Yes sir. If you would come with me please, I'll take you to the command center." Aaron was read his duties and expectations and was eager to carry them out. What he wasn't expecting was the level of technology in the room that was now to be his domain. As Aaron looked around, Ryan began to brief him on a new task force being assembled. They were gathering agents for a total Black Ops squad. Connor set up the large projector screen and put the first folder in front of Aaron. "Your first operative, assuming he agrees, is Commander Reese Kelly. He is a retired Navy Seal. Second in command will be Captain Bill Wright, retired from the Army Rangers and a Black Ops specialist. Third, we have Captain Janie Grisham—Black Ops tech specialists, Ace pilot, and retired Marine. Last but not least, is BJ Rainey—sniper, gunnery sergeant, and retired Marine. You will notice that each of these individuals has served several tours and are highly trained in terrorism."

"Exactly what are we asking of these men and women? It seems that they have already given plenty to their country."

"Indeed. These four were hand-picked because they have no family, sir. You've been assigned to setup a task force that will stop the upward swing of modern day piracy."

"I've seen news reports over the last few years, but wasn't aware it had become such a problem."

"It has—a worldwide problem, sir. The latest occurrences have been off the Golf Coast, the ports of New Orleans, and several have been reported around Texas as well—Houston, Galveston, and Corpus Christi. However, the main threat has been off the coast of Somalia. The teams should be arriving shortly. The British Prime Minister will also be joining us with a four-man team of his own. If our men don't sign on, we have a secondary four ready for recruitment. Although, I don't think these people know how to say 'no', so I doubt we'll encounter such an issue."

Approximately thirty minutes later, all four of the intended recruits were seated around the table with briefs in front of them. As soon as Vice President Woods entered the room, they all stood at attention. He saluted each of them and asked them to be seated. After they had finished reviewing the brief, he reminded them that they were not under any obligation to accept such an assignment. But, if they did, they would be the first Black Ops squad of their kind. No one was ever to know of their connection to the White House—orders were only to come from Woods himself, or Ryan Connors.

"Please take your time in deciding. In one hour, we will meet with the British Prime Minister and his men," Aaron informed them. Without hesitation, they each stood and accepted.

"With all due respect, Vice President Woods, there is nothing to consider here. We're in." Aaron searched all of their faces and only found confirmation. Pride rushed through his veins. These were true heroes.

Chapter Two

A special aircraft was landing at Norfolk Base. Aboard the plane were Prime Minister Griffen and British Special Forces: Jake Fulton (retired commander), Shawn Mitchell (retired sergeant snipper), Sarah Mckinzle (retired lieutenant, expert in explosives and undercover intelligence), and Thomas Granger (retired captain and pilot, expert in hand-to-hand-combat). Prime Minister Griffen informed them that they had arrived at their new headquarters.

They were shown to a black SUV with blacked out windows—the driver was most likely secret service. The driver spoke not one word as he opened the doors of the vehicle for the agents. Even though traffic in DC was always bad, it seemed just a little bit worse today. Perhaps it was just because they British Special Forces agents were jetlagged and not used to such traffic. An hour later, they pulled up in front of an abandoned warehouse. Sarah took note of the surveillance system. *Impressive*, she thought to herself. What appeared to be an abandoned building was anything but. They took a lift down what felt like twenty or so floors. When the gate opened to release them, it was as if they were walking onto a state-of-the-art Twilight Zone set. There were fifteen to twenty young techs working feverishly in front of large screens. What they were actually doing was anyone's guess. They stood, admittedly a little taken aback, as two men approached them.

"Welcome. I am Aaron Woods, Vice President of the United States, and this is Ryan Connors. We are very pleased to have you here." The group was led over to a large conference table and introductions were made between both teams. "You've all been briefed on the specifics, I assume. Now, we will dig into the real facts and logistics of this mission. The people we are bringing in are now being considered amongst the most dangerous in the world. They are extremely well organized and have consultants in almost every country. They have a firm finger on the pulse of the shipping and trade industry. Their latest spree has resulted in them taking hostage of private yachts and cruise liners— the most recent being off the coast of Galveston, Texas. A multi-millionaire, his wife, two security officers, and their small ship crew have been taken. The yacht was boarded by at least six armed men. The crew and guards were killed. Both Mr. and Mrs. Carter were badly beaten, and it has been reported that his wife was raped right in front of him. They took the wife with them and are asking for ten million dollars' ransom. Jessica Carter is a British citizen with royal ties. I am working on getting Mr. Carter in here so that you can question him. All of his calls and mail are being sent here, then will be forwarded to your new headquarters in New Orleans.

"These men are pirates, and they are armed with heavy duty fire power; we're talking automatic weapons, mortars, rocket powered grenades, and dangerously high-tech gadgets. They have spies all over the place feeding them information constantly on cargo and routes. The most dangerous attacks are currently happening in the south seas of China and Somalia; however, the waters around the Gulf Coast and Hawaii are rapidly catching up. Annual loss to date—worldwide—is approximately thirteen to sixteen billion dollars. Previously, they would only hit anchored ships, but now, the occurrence of kidnapping on the high seas and asking for higher ransoms is becoming too common.

"Previous practice has been to release these individuals after they have been captured and questioned. This is no longer acceptable. Once captured, they are to be sent to Guantanamo Bay for special holding procedures. The London world headquarters of shipping and insurance is a hub for intelligence being fed to these pirates. Several of these groups have informants in London. This leaves the pirates with plenty of time and ample resources to plan their attacks. There average haul from their victims is two million, but it can add up to hundreds of millions once the ransoms are factored in.

"You all realize that this is as Black Ops as it gets. I will need all of your IDs and credit cards, cell phones, all of it. We've created new identities for each of you. Now that you know the full story, if any of you has a problem with what is happening here, now is the time to say so. Once you leave this room, only myself, Ryan, and the Prime Minister will know the truth about your mission." Aaron paused to allow them a moment to process the gravity of what they were signing themselves up for. It really came as no surprise to him when they all agreed with a proud salute.

"Good luck to you all. Our countries owe you so much already. Now, the rest of the world will join us in that debt of gratitude. I have no doubt that you will be successful. God speed."

Chapter Three

They were taken to a private air strip and boarded an unmarked jet. Ryan would be supervising their take-off.

"You understand that, if you're caught, you're basically on your own?" He said addressing the group as one. "Although you will have your team to watch your back and get you out, you will have to learn to depend on each other because, as far as the rest of the world is concerned, you and this mission don't exist."

"Yes, sir." They declared in unison. They all settled into their seats and tried to prepare themselves for a little bit of sleep. Sarah stared out the window for a while, her thoughts reaching clear out across the ocean. She had divorced her husband of sixteen years and was still dealing with the emotional repercussions of it. She had to get her head in the game. This was exactly what she needed. She had missed her work in the service more than she thought. She was ready to give this one hundred percent. She looked around the cabin and silently profiled the others. Her perception of the group as a whole was that they would prove a force to be reckoned with. Deciding she wasn't ready to sleep quite yet, she opened her file and began to study it with a vengeance. Time was a major factor. If the ransom was not delivered soon, Mrs. Carter's chance of survival as slim.

Reese was also studying the file a few seats over. There wasn't a lot of information on the pirates themselves. It was unnerving how well organized they were as a group. His heart went out to their client, Mr. Carter. It must have been horrifying to witness the atrocities done to his wife—not knowing if she was now dead or alive. Despite the darkness surrounding this assignment, Reese hadn't felt this alive since his last mission with Seal Team Five. They all swore to keep in touch, but never did. They all had families and had easily settled into civilian life. *Best to leave the past in the past*, he thought. This was a new chapter and the closest he would get to another Navy mission.

Bill Wright was all too eager to hit the ground running. Of all the people on the plane, he had the most experience with the dark side of warfare. He loved Black Ops; he loved living on the edge. He loved cheating death. He would have liked to see his ex-wife and his three-year-old son before departing, but as far as they knew, he had died on his last mission. He had watched his own funeral from across the cemetery. It had been for their own good; he knew that. He had made some heavy-duty enemies over the years. He hadn't liked resigning his commission, but this seemed like a second chance for him to do what he was good at.

Gunnery sergeant BJ Rainey was one of the top ten snippers in the world, with over sixty confirmed kills. It was often hard for him to accept that he was no longer a front man in the Marines. But, at least now he had a place to use his expertise for the good of the world. BJ had no family left and had been a loner for much of his life. It might prove to be challenging for him to play nice as part of this team.

Captain Janie Grisham was coping with the death of both her parents due to a tragic car accident. She fully welcomed the distraction that this assignment would bring her. Maybe it would even be able to break her of her pesky drinking habit—getting rid of the pills would be a plus too. As a pilot in the Marines, she had flown over eighty missions over the course of her career. *I would really love to be flying this jet*, she thought to herself. Flying was the ultimate escape for her. It was the closet to God she was going to get, and she knew it. Janie had already studied the files, so she decided to get some sleep.

Jake Fulton was recently divorced with no children. His wife loved being married to a commander, but hated being married to him. Aside from his benefits and loyalty to the crown, he continuously signed up for missions to get away from her. At least on the front lines he was able to fight back.

Shawn Mitchel and Thomas Granger had served together and gone to university together. Once they had caught up with one another and hashed out old times, they both fell into a comfortable sleep.

Chapter Four

They landed on a private air strip deep in the swamps. It used to be a drug lord's compound, and now, it would serve as their base of operations. It was well hidden and well furnished. The group made their way inside and were surprised to see that it looked like a grand hotel. A man named Sherman led them to their rooms and told them that they would be briefed in six hours' time. Sarah's room was next to Reese's, with Janie on the other side. Reese couldn't sleep, so he went down the hall to the study. Sarah was already in there looking over intel reports.

"Hi. Are those new reports?"

"Yes. No calls yet on the ransom drop, but they still have several hours before the demand time."

"So, you couldn't sleep either huh?"

"No. It always takes me a few days to settle into a new time change."

"Yeah, that was always the hardest part about deployment for me too." Sarah handed Reese a stack of papers, and they continued to review the information in a comfortable silence. After a short while, one of the attendants entered the room and announced that Mr. Carter would be arriving within the hour. Reese went to wake the others.

Thomas was the next to enter the study. He actually looked well rested. As the rest of the group trickled in, they took a seat around the large table in the center of the room. A man entered with cups and a coffee pot. He set them up and left the room in silence. Shawn was the last to arrive. Ten minutes later, Matthew Carter joined them and told his body guards to wait in the other room. Immediately, Matt asked if there was any new news about his wife. They assured him that they would do all they could to bring her home safely and get those responsible for her harm behind bars for the rest of their lives.

Mr. Carter and his guards left for the evening, and the man who had brought in the coffee earlier reappeared to announce that dinner was ready in the formal dining hall. None of the agents were used to treatment like this. Normally, they were just grateful to have a tent in some godforsaken desert.

Conversation was light until dinner was served; that's when they strategically began to map out their plans. Ryan showed up halfway through the meal and asked if everything in the compound was meeting their needs so far. They all agreed that the accommodations were wonderful. After dinner, the group decided to turn in for the evening so that they could get an early start in the morning.

Ryan asked Reese and Sarah to join him for a night cap.

"So, how is everything going so far?"

"You don't have to worry, sir. Whoever picked this team had great insight. We are all playing nicely together," Reese told him. They all laughed and enjoyed the sense of comrade in the air. Ryan let them know that he was flying back to Washington to have a meeting with Vice President Woods, but ensured that he would be back before things got underway.

After Ryan left, Sarah decided that she was finally ready to get some sleep. She wished Reese a goodnight as he poured himself another drink. Reese sat there staring into this drink for a while, pondering their team. *This is a good group*, he thought, *no weak links*. These were men and women that he could trust with his life, and he had a feeling that that would prove to come in handy.

Chapter Five

The next morning, Janie made her way downstairs and into the dining hall. The only other person up already was Jake. He stood and offered her a chair. She thanked him and poured herself some coffee. They sat in silence for a few moments before Jake asked her what she thought they could expect in the day ahead. The others filtered in just as breakfast was being served. Thomas commented gratefully on the sleeping quarters and the quality of the chow.

"I could absolutely get used to this," he said through a mouthful of fresh-baked, buttery croissant.

"Sure beats the hell out of a cot in the middle of the desert," Sarah said.

"Most definitely," Shawn agreed. As they were finishing up, a man with a thick Cajun accent entered and asked when they would be ready for their tour of the compound. They promised to meet him in the foyer in fifteen minutes.

Once they had gathered, Jako asked what they would like to see first.

"We can start at the training center, weapons room, or my personal favorite, the garage where all of the cars and boats are kept," Jako suggested. The men in the group simultaneously agreed that they would like to see the toys first. Stepping into the large warehouse was like walking into an expensive showroom. There were tobacco boats that were all about speed, a fifty-foot yacht, and several stealth boats. All of the cars in the warehouse had been confiscated by the D.E.A.

"Mr. Connor's said that you are free to pick out your personal cars, but the boats are for assignments only," their tour guide told them. Janie went straight for the Porsche. Jake and Reese opted for a Land Rover, and BJ took the Jeep Wrangler. Bill chose the Ford 150, and Shawn was all over the Ferrari. Sarah went for the BMW, and Thomas got behind the wheel of the other Jeep. They were like kids in a candy store on Christmas. "Wait until you guys see the arsenal," Jako announced smiling at their enthusiasm. They toured the yacht which had a master bedroom with two beds, four additional state rooms, and on deck sat a massive fifty caliber machine gun mounted on the bow. There was also a rocket launcher rigged to an impressive lift, so that it could be hidden with the push of a button. The yacht was equipped with all of the latest gadgets and weaponry from the best in the world. Looking at it from across the water, you would think that it was a normal vessel.

The next stop was the arsenal. "I think you will all like this very much." He pushed open the double doors and Shawn and BJ simultaneously let out low whistles. This was a snippers Heaven on

Earth. They spent over an hour handling all of the guns and carefully choosing their personal weapons.

Finally, they made it into the training center. "In your rooms, you will find tactical wear and underwater clothes. Some of your training will obviously need to be on water. Ladies, I hope you like what was picked out for you. If not, I can take you into town so that you can pick out something that may be more pleasing to you."

It was almost noon by the time they made it back to the main compound. They were told that lunch would be served in fifteen minutes on the main terrace by the pool. None of them had ever experienced such luxury. Their lunch consisted of a shrimp casserole jambalaya, mud bugs, and fried alligator with red beans and rice. Sarah was a little leery of the fare, but she gave it the old English try and found it absolutely delicious. She couldn't bring herself to try the mud bugs though; she just couldn't get passed the eyes. Janie lifted her Bloody Mary to her lips and gasped for breath. The waiter chuckled and got her a glass of water. He had tried to warn her that they made them hot. Reese ended up finishing the drink for her.

It doesn't take long for the humidity to get to you when you aren't used to it. Shortly after lunch was over, they retired to their rooms. Sarah went into her room and opened the closet doors; her mouth fell open in surprise. Inside were designer gowns, dresses for day and evening wear, and all of the necessary accessories to go with—handbags, jewelry, shoes. Suddenly, there was a knock at her door. Sarah opened it and was greeted by a woman, named Tracy, who said that she would be her maid. Sarah couldn't believe what she was hearing. She never would have expected treatment like this when she accepted the mission.

Janie was in her quarters making the same discoveries, except she was actually trying on the dresses too. She was greeted by a woman, named Roxy, who would be seeing to her needs during her stay in the compound.

The men weren't as excited about the new clothes, even though their closets were filled with Armani suits and Rolex watches. Reese and Jake met downstairs and headed over to the exercise room. Thomas and BJ were already there. Shawn and Bill were in the pool. After their romp in the gym, Jake asked Jako where they might be able to go out for at least a five mile run.

"I don't recommend leaving the compound until you know the terrain better. Alligators, pythons, and quick sand can sneak up on you quickly when you are unfamiliar with your surroundings. I'll scout out some possible routes for you tomorrow. Dinner will be served at seven in the formal dining room. Please dress appropriately for the occasion. Training begins tonight."

"What training?"

"To live like the rich and powerful."

"I think we are all adapting nicely."

Yes, but you can still tell that this is unfamiliar to you. The training will be to make it seem as if you expect nothing less."

"This is awesome. We are going to be dressed to the nines, living large, and still end up shot." They all laughed at Jake's comment. Jako did not see the humor in being shot and that just made it all the more amusing. They would have an hour and a half to get ready for their formal dinner training.

Chapter Six

Their respective maids and valets were waiting for them when they arrived at their rooms. Sarah and Janie simultaneously stood in front of the mirrors in their rooms, stunned at their own reflections. *Where is the tomboy I used to be*, Sarah thought to herself. *Who knew this is what I was hiding under those uniforms all this time.* Janie was having similar thoughts about her own appearance. She may not have considered herself a tomboy, but she had never been given the chance to look like this.

The ladies were fashionably late, so the men had already gathered at the bottom of the staircase. As the women made their way down the stairs, six pairs of eyes followed their every move. *This is better than senior prom*, Janie laughed to herself. Sarah was so nervous; all she could think about was putting one foot in front of the other. She glanced up for only a second and immediately met Reese's eyes. All thoughts, about her feet or otherwise, vanished. She felt as though they were the only two people in the world. A low whistle from one of the other men quickly brought her back to reality. Reese looked over at BJ like he wanted to strangle him.

Dinner was not at all what they were expecting. It was not the light atmosphere they had already grown accustomed to during mealtime, because they were all being forced to practice a very particular set of manners. Jako seemed surprisingly at ease.

"I was raised in France with my wealthy grandmother. The etiquette I learned there has served me well over the years."

They enjoyed an exquisite ten course meal. After dinner, they went to the study for cocktails. "Don't stay up too late. Breakfast is at five o'clock and training starts at six-thirty," Jako advised like a protective father. BJ and Shawn followed him out. The rest of the group opted for another night cap.

They settled into an easy discussion of all things to come. This was by far the most elaborate mission any of them had ever been assigned to. After their glasses were emptied, the rest of the group turned in; but Reese wasn't ready yet. He made himself comfortable behind one of the desks and began reviewing their files, outlining their best options for success. He stayed at it for a little over an hour before he decided that no more could be done until they received further instruction from Mrs. Carter's kidnappers. As he turned the corner to ascend the stairs, he noticed Sarah on her way down.

"We've really got to stop meeting like this. People will start to talk," he joked.

"I'm just grabbing another book to read," she laughed. He bid her goodnight and went upstairs. Sarah watched him until he reached the top, then continued to the library.

Chapter Seven

The team started their day with a five mile run, then split into groups for the remainder of the training session. BJ and Shawn went to the arsenal and picked out long-range rifles, then headed out for some target practice. Janie and Thomas went to the air field to practice helicopter maneuvers. Sarah and Jake were in the training center making bombs. In another corner of the center, Bill and Reese were practicing hand-to-hand combat and stealth in water. Jako observed each group at their stations and kept a close eye out for gators. They took turns rotating through each training station so that they would develop expertise in all areas. Four hours later, they called it a day and returned to their rooms to get cleaned up for lunch.

Reese caught up with Sarah and Jake. "Hey guys. How'd it go?" he asked.

"Good! It feels great to have a purpose again doesn't it?" Sarah replied.

"Hell yeah it does." Reese confirmed.

Lunch today was a mixture of southern and Cajun cuisine. Talk was light today, as they all realized how much training had taken out of them. Jako suggested that they focus on inside Ops for the remainder of the afternoon.

"Why haven't we been there yet?" Sarah asked.

"I wanted to save the best for last," Jako replied with a smirk. After the lunch break, they all piled into an elevator. When they stepped out, it was like nothing they had ever seen before. It even put their headquarters in Washington to shame. The walls were made out of a thick glass, and the chamber was pressurized. Two servicemen were guarding a door that Jako opened without a word being passed between them. As they walked through the door, Sarah's eyes grew wide in amazement. This was a computer nerd's paradise. Jako introduced them to a man named Simon Westmore. He was the lead technician of the compound.

"I will be back to retrieve you in two hours," Jako told them. Until their security badges arrived, he would have to escort them to the secured areas within the compound. Sarah and Janie had already begun to wander curiously. Jako let the men know that they could ask Simon if they needed anything.

There was a room specifically for forensics, and another room that acted as the command center to keep them in communication with the Washington Ops center. Bill and Sarah opted to stay in the command center and learn about the various things the techs were working on. They had collected quite a bit of data on the pirates' movements and were monitoring everything having to do with the Carters in real-time. The group was so immersed in all they were learning, that the hours passing only felt like minutes.

Before they knew it, Jako had returned and informed them that Ryan would be joining them for dinner this evening. The team was working well together and after just 48 hours, it felt like they had been a cohesive team for years. As they made their way up the stairs to get ready for dinner, Sherman—the compound's respected butler—announced that Ryan and Mr. Carter were already waiting for them in the library and that dinner would be served in an hour.

Sarah took a quick shower and had her maid help her with her hair. She picked out a chic black dress and jewels to match. She couldn't help but think again how good it felt to have a schedule again, a purpose, something to focus on. Reese and Sarah left their rooms at the same time.

"May I walk you down?" he asked.

"Yes, of course." She placed her hand in the crook of his arm, and together they walked quietly down the stairs. As they entered the library, Ryan offered them a drink. They settled into easy conversation as the rest of the group trickled in. Once everyone had arrived, they made their way to the dining hall. Dinner exceeded everyone's expectations and the conversation was engaging despite the weight of Mrs. Carter's kidnapping. After dinner, they made their way to the study for coffee and cocktails. Jako suddenly rushed in and said that Mr. Carter had a call. They all rushed to the command center to receive the call so that they could attempt to trace the kidnappers' location.

"How do I even know my wife is still living? I'm not sending you a dime until you let me talk to her, until I know she's okay," Carter demanded. The line grew quiet for a moment. Carter's heart raced faster with each passing second.

"Matt?" His wife's voice sounded frail.

"Jess…oh my god, Jessie are you okay honey?"

"Hurry, please hurry Matt," she begged.

"I will contact you tomorrow with further instruction. Make sure I get what I want," came the harsh rasp of the kidnapper's voice. Then, the line went dead.

"We weren't able to get a trace. They must be using a satellite phone," Janie announced. Mr. Carter's face couldn't decide if it wanted to show relief or devastation. He felt like he could breathe again knowing that she was still alive, but that breath was sucked right back out of his body as he realized that she might not be for much longer. Ryan looked around the room and told the team to be up early the next day. They had quite a bit of training to accomplish before they would be ready to make the exchange with the kidnappers.

Reese, Sarah, and Jake remained in the study for a while longer to work on strategic maneuvers that they wanted to practice the next day. They composed a detailed list and made copies for the rest of the team.

Chapter Eight

The next morning, the team ate a quick breakfast and went over the schedule for the day. Ryan requested that Jako meet him in the office for a quick word.

"Tell me honestly, Jako, what have you observed with this group?"

"Honestly, sir, they are the best that I have ever seen."

"That says a lot coming from you, Jako." Jako just grinned at Ryan's comment. He and Ryan went way back, and they trusted each other's opinions greatly.

Mr. Carter was out on the patio watching the team as they trained and trying to get some of his own work done. He was having little success as his thoughts wandered uncontrollably. Ryan ended up joining him a little while later and they discussed the tremendous potential of this team. There was no denying it, they were good.

Lunch was a hurried affair as the team eagerly awaited the call from the pirates. They enjoyed ribeye steaks and Alaskan crab legs, with soup and salad and shrimp cocktails as starters. Sarah was again amazed by their luck in accepting this mission. Even though they were living the life now, in the back of her mind, Sarah knew that things were about to get really real. She looked over at Reese, and as if he knew what she was thinking, he lifted his glass in a silent toast. She responded with the same gesture.

Simon entered and told Ryan that he had a call on the secure line. It was Vice President Woods requesting an update.

"To put it simply, they are amazing sir. I have full faith that they will bring great success to this mission and any others that we throw at them."

Later that afternoon, they had all gathered in the command center in anticipation of the call. Waiting was always the worst part of any operation. The call came in right on time; everyone listened intently. Mr. Carter was instructed to meet a ship in the international waters off the coast of New Orleans at six o'clock sharp the next evening. He was to have no more than two guards on board with him.

"Ten million in exchange for your wife," the kidnapper said callously. "Any sign of the police and you and your wife will be shot on the spot. No exceptions." Mr. Carter said that he understood the conditions. After the line was disconnected, the team went right out to rig up the sail boat for the mission. BJ and Thomas would act as Mr. Carter's two guards. Janie and Bill would pilot the two small subs on board and the other four would discreetly attempt to board the pirate vessel. They had orders to use extreme measures if necessary.

They prepared their weapons and scuba gear, along with waterproof ear wicks and night vision goggles. By the time they finally made it back to the compound for dinner, they were as prepared as they could possibly be for this mission. After dinner, Reese and Sarah went to the study to finalize their plans. After about an hour, they decided that the most valuable thing they could do at this point was get some sleep. Sarah crawled into bed and was able to fall asleep without any trouble. Reese, on the other hand, paced his room for another hour or so, which was his normal habit before a big mission.

Chapter Nine

The next day, tension over the mission was high. They were grateful to have the benefit of the darkness to assist them. It would make the element of surprise much easier, especially because the subs couldn't be picked up on any radar system. Jako would be playing the part of Mr. Carter tonight—much to the dislike of the real Mr. Carter; he did not like the idea of being left behind.

The team made last minute inspections as the time grew near. It would take them two hours to sail to the coordinates the pirates had requested. Once they were ten miles out, they tested communication with each other and Ryan back at command. Everything was a go.

BJ spotted the pirate ship approaching on the horizon. He counted at least eight men on board—very heavily armed, and there was no telling how many more were below deck. BJ told everyone to hold their position and to get Mr. Carter in a life raft with the money. Ryan gave the order to engage. Reese, Sarah, Shawn, and Jake silently boarded the ship and immediately took out two guards on the starboard side. They waited, hidden, until Mrs. Carter had been loaded into the life raft with four other men. Jako held his position. BJ and Thomas were ready to take out the men in the raft. Reese and Sarah made their way around one side of the pirate vessel while Jake and Shawn went around the other side.

Everything seemed to be going smoothly until they discovered that it wasn't Mrs. Carter in the raft. Jako subtly made the call telling Sarah and the others to search the ship. Sarah covered Reese's back as they made their way down an interior corridor. It seems almost too quiet. They found it unlikely that the pirates they obtained on deck were the only ones on board. Suddenly, they heard muffled voices coming from the end of the hallway. Reese turned around put a finger to his lips, letting Sarah know that silence was mandatory. They crept closer, each taking a defensive stance on either side of the door. Jake and Shawn joined them and waited for the signal.

Suddenly, they heard the handle to the heavy door unlatch and a man stepped out. Sarah smashed the butt of her rifle into the side of his jaw and had him cuffed before he even hit the floor at her feet. Reese, Jake, and Shawn rushed into the room, sending bullets into the six other bodies that came forward in attack. Only two of the seven men were killed; the rest suffered surface wounds that rendered them useless in resisting arrest. Jake and Shawn moved the five detained pirates to the hallway while Sarah hurried to Jessica Carter's side, releasing her from her binds and checking her condition.

Aside from some superficial injuries and obvious emotional trauma, Sarah deemed her well enough to make it back to the boat on her own two feet. The three made their way back to the ship with their captives.

"Who's the woman?" Jako asked Mrs. Carter as they cruised back to the mainland.

"Her name is Kat. She saved my life. When they were beating me, she got in the way. They did horrible things to her. Where's my husband?"

"He's back at the compound. We have medical staff standing by."

"Sir, I don't think this woman can wait for medical attention," Janie said from below deck before she went to grab her medical bag. Before she went back down, she stopped in front of Mrs. Carter and began to check her vitals.

"I'm fine. Please, take care of Kat first," Mrs. Carter insisted.

"With all due respect, ma'am, you are our first priority. I will do the best that I can to help that woman, but I need to be able to tell your husband how you are doing." Jako approached and gave Janie the okay to go below and see to the other woman. Janie complied. Looking over the woman, Janie was saddened to see that she was more dead than she was alive.

"What did they do to you?" Janie whispered to her. She started an IV and got some fluids going. Her breathing was so shallow that Janie didn't think she would even make it to port without the help of a breathing tube. "I need some help down here!" she called up to those on deck. Reese came down and collected hair samples and fingerprints from the young woman so that they could attempt to find out who she was and where she came from.

Back at the command center, Ryan had received the fingerprints and immediately ran them through CODIS. *Good God*, he thought, then immediately turned to warm the medical staff about what they were up against. They were all ready and standing by. Carter told them to do whatever was necessary to save the woman that saved his wife.

An hour later, the sail boat arrived back at the private dock. Mrs. Carter and Kat were carried on gurneys to the medical ward. Mr. Carter ran over to his wife and took her hand. Tears streamed down his faced as he pressed her palm to his lips. He didn't let go of her the entire time she was being examined and treated. The doctor informed him that, although they still had tests to run on both women, Mrs. Carter seemed to have nothing more than a few bumps and bruises. Kat was being rushed into surgery.

Reese and Sarah followed Jako and Ryan into the command center, while the rest of the team unloaded the ship and got their gear put away. Kat ended up being in surgery for several hours. When the surgeon finally came out, he said that the rest was up to God. The pirates that had been captured were being held in cells underneath the compound. They would be flown to Guantanamo Bay the following day where they would basically disappear. The entire team met in the command center to go over each aspect of the mission and discuss what could have gone better. Everyone seemed to be in agreement that the raid had been seamless and everyone had contributed to the best of their abilities.

The conversation eventually turned to this mystery woman. They wondered what kind of secrets she would reveal once she was in recovery. Ryan planned to meet with Jessica the next morning to debrief her. Reese, Sarah, and Jake would go down to interrogate the prisoners before they were released from the compound. Mr. and Mrs. Carter were allowed to head home for the night. Jessica made each of them promise to do whatever they could for Kat. Sarah understood the kind of bond that could form in circumstances like what these two women had just been through. Ryan instructed them all to get some rest and congratulated them on a job well done.

Janie wandered into the study and fixed herself a vodka on the rocks. She knew she wouldn't be able to get much sleep tonight. She was never able to sleep after a mission. Her body just wouldn't allow her to process the adrenaline that quickly.

Chapter Ten

The pirates left nothing identifiable on Kat's body, making a database search useless. All of her teeth had been pulled out and her fingertips and been burned to mask any worthwhile print. Every bone in her body had been broken over the span of a four to five-month period, according to the surgeon. This woman had been put through unspeakable torture and just thrown away as a decoy. It was a miracle in itself that she had even survived this long. Jake couldn't stop thinking about her.

Around two o'clock in the morning, Jake crept down to the hospital ward to sit with her. He just watched her for the longest time; his heart breaking with every artificial breath she took. He ended up falling asleep in the chair next to her bed, holding her hand gently. He had never considered himself to be any kind of sentimental, but something about this woman touched the depths of his heart.

Sarah came in later that morning and sent him back up to his room, promising to stay with Kat for a while. She carried on a friendly one-way conversation with her for a little while. When the doctor came in to check her vitals, he assured Sarah that this young woman was holding her own; she had already proven her ability and desire to survive. There was no way of knowing how much damage to her brain had been done until she woke up; if she woke up. A nurse came in to change her gown and give her some fresh bed sheets. Sarah noticed a small tattoo on Kat's left shoulder. It was a delicate black and white rose with a date below it in old English lettering. She snapped a quick photo. Maybe this could help them figure out who she was.

Jake had spent most of the day reading to Kat. He made the medical staff promise not to leave her alone—not even for a minute. The whole team was taking turns sitting with her, and even the Carters had been by to check on her progress. The swelling in her face had gone down considerably and some of her older bruises were beginning to heal. Although there weren't yet any signs of her waking from the coma, the doctors were convinced that she was being kept alive by the sheer will of the team.

Jako called them all into the study to let them know that they had been invited to a gala hosted by one of the suspected leaders of the pirate clans. Apparently, the stories that had been spun about their new identities, and leaked into the underworld, had been convincing. It was time to really put their training, and acting skills, to the test. Reese and Sarah would act as a wealthy couple known for selling weaponry on the black market. Janie and Janie would act as bodyguards, while BJ would be their trusty limo driver. Thomas, Shawn, and Bill would manage surveillance. There was a sense of excitement throughout the room. Their watches and jewelry concealed an incredible array of technology that could pass through any security system without being detected.

The man hosting the party, Camron Mendoza, had a long history selling drugs, people, and guns. It looked like his newest business venture was pirating. That night, Sarah and Janie let their maids work their feminine magic on them. They both discreetly and securely strapped several guns and blades to the inside of their thighs.

Their limo pulled up to the front of an impressive French mansion not far from Bourbon street in the French Quarter. The doors to the limo were opened by tuxedo clad servants. The group was shown up the magnolia lined driveway by a majordomo. Sarah thought it was one of the most beautiful drives that she had ever seen. There was a certain magic about this place that she couldn't quite put her finger on, good or bad. They went through a metal detector and surrendered their weapons along with their coats.

The party was already in full swing. They were escorted to a large table on the far side of the room. Mendoza approached shortly after they had made themselves comfortable. Reese shook his hand and politely introduced Sarah as his wife. Mendoza held Sarah's hand for just a moment too long, which did not go unnoticed by Reese. He was surprised by how genuinely these jealous feelings arose in him. Luckily, it played in perfectly with his cover.

Reese knew better than to rush into talks of business. He kept their discussion friendly until Mendoza asked Sarah if she would honor him with a dance. While Sarah danced with Mendoza, Reese led a woman named Jeanette on the dance floor. Soon, several other guests joined them. The guest list was an impressive array of local and government officials. There were also several who Reese knew for a fact were on the 'most wanted' list.

Janie and Jake were sending a consistent stream of photos back to command.

"So, how are you liking New Orleans?" Mendoza asked Sarah. She answered politely, but couldn't help noticing that he continued to ask subtle questions about her 'husband's' business dealings. She was ready with her answers and smiled all the while.

Dinner was nothing short of extravagant. There was hot creole crab dip, creole baked cheese rice, a shrimp and lobster bisque, and tomato salad with a main course of beef tenderloin steaks in a creole spice rub, French cod, and hush puppies. And, of course, there was an impressive Bloody Mary bar with the specialty local hot bean. Sarah was more than aware of Mendoza's eyes on her throughout dinner. After the Banana Fosters and Brandy Alexanders, everyone returned the dancefloor. The festivities went on until two in the morning.

Reese and Sarah bid a courteous goodbye to their host and made their way back to the limo. When they arrived at the compound, they decided that they would sleep first and debrief in the morning. Jake went down to check on Kat before calling it a night.

"What is it about you?" he asked her, knowing that he wouldn't receive an answer. Maybe it was her courage, or maybe it was just because she seemed so alone, and alone was a feeling he knew well.

Chapter Eleven

Ryan was on his way to brief Vice President Woods on the results of the Carter rescue and the previous night's gala.

"The gala was a great success. The tech team had a field day with all of the photos being sent over. The place was crawling with people that have been on our radar and even more people that probably should be on our radar. The information we received from surveillance alone was monumental."

"That's fantastic news. And what of the young woman from the ship?"

"Still no match."

"I have a name for you to contact. It seems your inquiries have sent up a red flag. His name is Carl Radford."

"So this involves the CIA?"

"I'm afraid so. He's awaiting your call."

"I'll handle it as soon as we are done here, sir."

"How is the young woman recovering?"

"She's still in a coma, but the team has been keeping a close eye on her. If she awakes, we will have another great asset."

"Agreed." The men finished their meal and Ryan headed to the Washington Monument. Radford was already waiting for him with a file in hand.

"So how's the spook business Carl?"

"No different than when you were here Ryan. I hope you've been well."

"I heard you found my missing girl?"

"It would appear so."

"You know, if she wakes up, I'll have to debrief her."

"Yes, if she wakes up."

"Is that her file?"

"Yep. I hope she does wake up. She's a good agent."

"For you to say that she must really be something special."

"She is brother."

"Well, I'll keep you in the loop."

"I appreciate it. I'll look forward to hearing from you. Goodnight."

"Goodnight Carl. Thank you."

Meanwhile, Connor's chopper was landing. Jako was waiting for him on the helo pad. The team were all out on the yard training. They really took their workouts seriously.

"How is the girl?" Connor asked.

"Unfortunately, there has been no change sir."

"At least she isn't getting any worse. Has there been any word from Mendoza?"

"Yes actually, he requested a business meeting with Reese for tomorrow afternoon."

"Excellent." That meant that everything was right on track. "Here is the file on Kat. We will brief the team at dinner."

"Of course, sir. See you then." Jako said with a salute. Ryan went down to check on Kat, then made his way over to command to see how things were going. A little while later, the entire team arrived in command at the request of Ryan.

"Vice President Woods is very pleased with the work you all are doing," Ryan praised. "The files I am handing you now are on Kat. We will review and discuss over dinner. Go ahead and get ready. I will see you all again shortly."

As soon as Jake made it back to his room, he immediately opened the file on Kat. *So our mystery girl is a spook*, he thought to himself. She had been under deep cover for over two years. Apparently, she went on record as being missing nearly six months ago; clearly her cover had been blown. She was so strong. Jake didn't know many who could withstand the same things she had gone through. He had never considered himself a religious man, but he found himself praying for her. He figured, *it can't hurt right?*

After dinner, the group retired to the study to discuss Kat and the recent chatter coming in regarding the pirates. They weren't exactly sure what role Mendoza played, but they certainly couldn't rule him out as a low level pawn. Even though kidnapping and ransom hadn't been his MO in the past, it was becoming the fastest way for these people to make some real money. Once the briefing was complete, Jake went down to the hospital to sit with Kat until Janie came down to relieve him around four in the morning. The rest of the group retired for the night.

Chapter Twelve

The Mendoza meeting was scheduled for noon on the west end of Bourbon Street, which always seemed to be dark and dank—even on the brightest of days. You could buy anything from drugs to dark magic on this end of the street. Mendoza was waiting for Reese at the back of a strip club. The patrons frequenting this club were lost souls—the strippers included. One of them came up to Reese and wrapped her arms around his neck.

"Hey there handsome. With a face like that you can have whatever you want."

"That's a very generous offer, but I'm not sure my wife would approve."

"I won't tell if you won't," she said with a dangerous grin.

"Look he said he wasn't interested okay. Get lost," Jake said, playing the role of body guard perfectly. He took her arm and put some distance between her and Reese. Mendoza stood up and told his own guards to clear the club.

"Reese, so good to see you again. I'm glad that we had a chance to do this."

"What can I do for you?" Reese asked. Mendoza sat back down and gestured for them to do the same.

"I have a need for some automatic rifles, and I've heard that you have a few that you'd like to get off your hands. We'll start there."

"How many are we talking?"

"One hundred cases of ten. Clips and ammo too."

"What's your price? If we can come to reasonable terms, then I have some other products that you might be interested in." Mendoza grinned and gave him a low-ball, one-time fee. Reese agreed without much negotiation and they worked out a pick up location out in the swamps. New Orleans was still a smugglers paradise. Not much had changed since Jean Laffite's day. In fact, the compound they were currently using as headquarters was probably his lair.

"The exchange will take place in two days' time," Reese told Ryan once they were back at the compound. It was going to be a busy two days as the team prepared to put yet another dent in the pirate's network. The gang excelled when preparing for a mission. This is truly what they lived for. The adrenaline coursed through their veins, causing them to feel alive and needed by the country that had given them so much.

Just then, news from command came in that there was an attack suspected to take place on an incoming cargo ship. They were close enough that they may actually be able to intercept the attack. They located a cove where they could see the cargo ship come in without being detected. They also had a clear view of any other incoming ships. They had been in place for only an hour when the cargo ship came into view. The pirates' ship was right on its heels, ready to attack. The team was dressed in black and ready to board the cargo ship. They worked together, as one unit, and opened fire. The team was able to apprehend the pirates that had already boarded the cargo ship. They killed eight and injured five. They left the dead and brought the injured pirates back to their boat. The prisoners were blindfolded as the team made their way back to the compound. Once they reached port, the captured were taken down to the holding cells.

Later that evening, over a light dinner, the group joked about how this would probably be the last easy mission they would see. If the pirates were smart, they would begin taking more precautions. It didn't matter though; this team was ready for anything.

As they were finishing up their meal, Simon suddenly came running into the room.

"She's awake! She's awake!" The team jumped up immediately, nearly over turning the table, and ran for the elevators. She was in fact awake, but you could see the confusion etched in her face. Jake approached her slowly so that he wouldn't frighten her.

"Where am I?" She asked, her voice gravely. "Where's Jessica? Is she alright?"

"Yes, she's okay. Thanks to you. You are both safe now," Jake assured her.

"How long have I been in here?"

"About two weeks."

"Your voice sounds so familiar."

"Yes, I spent a lot of time sitting with you and talking to you while you were in the coma. We all did," he said gesturing to the rest of the group. "Do you feel up to talking about what happened? We already know that you were under cover for a long time." Just then, the doctor entered and told them that she truly needed to rest and get her bearings before questioning began. They left her and returned to their rooms. Jake showered and returned to the ward to find Kat napping. He sat down in the chair next to her bed and just watched her sleep. She had the most beautiful green eyes he had ever seen. He hoped that his draw to her would lessen now that she was awake, but something told him that it wasn't going to.

Kat awoke again. This time, the dark haired woman with the English accent was sitting where the man named Jake had been. Her mind felt so jumbled by all of the thoughts that were trying to be processed in her mind. She could almost swear that she remembered this woman. She was the one who had helped Jessica. Suddenly, Kat had mental flashes of being beaten, then everything just went black. She thought she heard people talking while she was stuck under the darkness, but if there was one voice she was sure she recognized, it was Jake's.

"Hi Kat. Do you remember me? My name is Sarah," the British woman said. Kat tried to speak, but her throat was still so sore that it made her voice a raspy whisper. "It's okay. You don't have to say anything. You need your rest. There is plenty of time to talk once you have your strength back," Sarah said, offering her a gentle smile. A nurse came in to check Kat's vitals and administered her scheduled dose of pain medication. It didn't take long for the meds to knock her right back out.

Reese came in and found Sarah still sitting with Kat as she slept. He was pleased to hear from Sarah that Kat seemed to be improving.

"Come on kid. Let's join the others for breakfast," Reese told her, extending his hand.

"Shouldn't someone stay with her?" She asked before taking his hand and allowing him to help her up.

"She'll be fine. She will be under the influence of all those pain meds for quite a few hours yet. You on the other hand, need to eat." Sarah smiled at the care in his voice.

When they arrived in the dining hall, Ryan and the rest of the team were just sitting down. Sarah filled them all in on what the nurse had told her about Kat's condition.

"If she is able to regain her full memory, she will be able to give us intimate details on these bastards," Ryan said.

"She might not want to join us. Did you think about that? Not after all she has been through," said Jake.

"That may be so, and that would be her choice. We won't force her into anything she isn't ready or willing for."

Chapter Thirteen

The team was just finishing up their routine run when Jako called them into the command center.

"Mendoza has invited you to join him in his box at the Super Dome for a New Orleans Saints game," Jako announced. Reese was more than pleased to get this news.

"I've always been more of a soccer girl myself," Sarah said.

"That's perfect!" Ryan laughed. "That will fit perfectly into your cover. Use that. Plan this one out to the T you two. With a man like Mendoza, we can't afford any mistakes." Jake and Janie would again play the role of bodyguards for the well-to-do couple.

"I even recommend that the two of you go out and spend the day in the city. Let yourselves be seen as a normal couple. The less suspicious Mendoza is of you, the better chance we have of pulling all this off," Ryan suggested. The group finished their lunch and prepared to do just that.

Sarah had no idea what one wears on 'an outing in the city' so she left that detail up to her maid—who executed perfectly as expected. As she was coming down the stairs to meet Reese, his breath was taken away by the woman before him—

even in simple day clothes. He offered his hand to help her down the last couple of steps and smiled at her in a way that made her blush.

They took the limo into town, accompanied by their 'bodyguards'. Ryan watched them drive off from one of the terraces at the compound. He was still in awe at how good they were at undercover work. What exceptional luck they'd had in selecting this team.

With the others in town for the rest of the afternoon, Jake wandered down to the hospital ward. He was pleased to see Kat awake and trying to eat. He took the fork and helped her finish the last few bites. She seemed grateful to have his help, but a little angry and embarrassed at the same time. She was sure that she was the type who didn't like to accept help very often. The nurse came in shortly after, took her tray, and gave her some medication. Once again, she was overcome by sleep, as was common because of the dosage.

When she awoke, there was a different man sitting at her bedside. She hadn't seen this man before; she was sure of it.

"Hello Kat. My name is Ryan Connors, and I am the Deputy Administrator to Vice President Woods. How are you feeling?"

"Honestly, there isn't a single place on my body that doesn't hurt. I'm so tired, but so sick of sleeping."

"I will see what I can do about having your medications adjusted. It might help alleviate some of that."

"Thank you…look, I don't remember much of anything. I just remember Jessica and the beatings.

"That's okay. Take your time. It will come to you. The doctor expects you to make a full recovery."

"This may sound strange…but I can't shake this feeling that I need to get back to something in my life—something really important—but I can't for the life of me think of what it is."

"That makes more sense to me than it does to you. Don't worry yourself. There will be plenty of time for all that when you are better. Get your rest. If there is anything that you remember, and you want to talk about it, don't hesitate to call," he said handing her his card. After leaving the hospital ward, Ryan made his way up to command to watch the live surveillance of Reese and Sarah. One of the techs informed him that there were two men that had been following them for a good hour now.

Of course Reese and Sarah had already figured out that they had picked up a tail, but that didn't stop them from playing the part of enthusiastic tourist. They strolled along Bourbon Street and perused the various shops. They even stopped at a quaint little café and ordered an appetizer to share. They checkout out a wonderful farmers' market and caught the trolley to a museum and an art gallery. Anyone watching would have no idea that they were anything other than a happy couple on vacation.

Just to ensure that they weren't followed back to the compound, Ryan arranged for them to stay at a townhouse in the French Quarter until the day of the football game. Early that evening, the couple received a dinner invitation to Emeril's restaurant. They were both astonished by the invitation seeing as how the waiting list was currently two years long.

The limo pulled up outside of the restaurant and Sarah and Reese made their way inside. They were immediately shown to their table, where Mendoza and a few of his men were waiting to join them. The mood was light, the food and wine was to die for, and there was absolutely no talk of business. The woman accompanying Mendoza this evening was stunningly beautiful, but she didn't say a word the entire time. Sarah was able to gather, in indirect conversation, that her name was Gabriella.

After dinner, Reese and Sarah were invited to Mendoza's club where they drank and danced the night away. Once they were back at the townhouse, Sarah sat for a moment and reflected on the evening. One thing was for sure, pirates sure know how to party.

Sarah wasn't sure why they had to share a room; all of their servants were in on the operation. But, I guess one couldn't be too careful when dealing with someone like Mendoza. They still hadn't been able to link him to the Somalian pirates, but they knew they would come across some breadcrumb eventually. If nothing else, Mendoza was a very dangerous man, and Ryan wanted to be able to nail him under enough charges to keep him put away for a very long time. Busting him on drugs and arms dealing wasn't enough. They wanted to pin him for human trafficking and kidnapping as well. Kat couldn't have been the only one. And after seeing what was done to her, they could only assume how many others hadn't been lucky enough to survive.

Sunday came way too soon for Sarah's taste. She wasn't entirely enthused about the idea of this football game, but Reese was ecstatic. *What is it with Americans and football?* She wondered inwardly. Mendoza had arranged it so that they were shown directly through security and up to his private box. There was an impressive feast displayed with lots and lots of champagne. Sarah could easily see how a lifestyle like this consumed people; the clothes, jewelry, and cars were all lovely, but she appreciated the simpler things, like a cottage in the country with no neighbors on either side. She plastered on her best smile before they entered the box and approached their host.

They saw a few of the same faces from the previous evening. Sarah was sure that they were the who's who of the criminal world. Reese, seeming to read her mind, just smiled and casually laced his fingers with hers in reassurance. Mendoza greeted them and kissed her available hand. He briefly introduced the other guests. It was early noon, and still twenty minutes until kickoff, but everyone in the box was already either drunk or high—or both. There appeared to be approximately a kilo of coke on the glass table in the middle of the small room. Mendoza led them over to the table and insisted that they try it, promising that the product was exceptional.

"The finest in America!" he boasted. They both indulged in a line and accepted a glass of champagne. By the second half of the game, the party was in full swing. Once Mendoza's attention was less focused on them, Reese and Sarah were able to turn down another line of coke without causing a scene, and the rest of their drinks ended up in the nearby planters around the room. The Saints were up 27-0 and spirits were high. Sarah noticed that Gabriella seemed like she was far away. She slowly made her way over to the young woman and asked her if something was the matter.

"I'm just tired," Gabriella said shrugging. By the time the game ended, the box had cleared itself out. Reese and Sarah thanked Mendoza for another fantastic time and made their way out to the limo. They would stay in the townhouse one more night, then head back to the compound early the next morning.

Chapter Fourteen

Back at the compound, Kat was getting stronger with each passing day. Jake would read to her and challenge her to games of chess. She was very good, but couldn't remember how she ever learned how to play. She was amazed by the things her brain chose to remember and the things that it insisted on forgetting. Although, the doctor still anticipated a full recovery.

"It will just take some time," everyone kept saying to her. It was so frustrating because it felt like time was the one thing that she didn't have. Ryan came in shortly after the doctor had left and asked if she felt up to talking.

"Sure," she answered, sitting up in bed a little more.

"Kat, you are a CIA, deep undercover agent. You have been working this assignment with the pirates for two years—mostly in Somalia. You had been off the grid for three months before my team got a hold of you. We took the ship that you were being held on with Jessica. Does any of this trigger anything in you?"

"Only the part about Jessica. I remember her."

"As soon as the doctor gives you the okay, your CIA case leader will come down to brief you on the details of your mission over the last two years. We're hopeful that it will spark some memories for you."

"I am hopeful too."

Back in D.C., Carl Radford was heading for a meeting with Absame Kubal. Every minute the man spent in this country placed him in jeopardy. The name Absame translated to 'the great one' and he very much tried to live up to the name. He was head of one of the largest terrorist organizations in the world.

"Carl, my friend, please tell me that you have found my woman," Absame said, shaking Carl's hand before they sat down.

"Yes, she is alive, but she has no memory of us at all."

"Carl, I will be clear…I want her dead."

"She was rescued by a team of total Black Ops. I don't have clearance, and therefore no access to her. They said that they will let me see her as soon as the doctor treating her gives the okay. We just need to be patient. Try not to worry, Absame. I will make sure she never remembers."

"Make sure that you do, otherwise your life will replace hers, my friend."

"Understood," Carl acknowledged as a chill ran down his spine. Kat had been one of the greatest assets the CIA had ever recruited. Unfortunately, she had been too good at her job. He hated the fact that he had to kill her. She had become like a daughter to him. But, when it came down to her life versus his, the choice became much easier.

Chapter Fifteen

Jake couldn't sleep so he went down to Kat's room. The nurse told him that she was also restless tonight. Jake went in and sat with her. They eased into conversation about her past and what he did as a member of this Black Ops team. Suddenly, as if someone had struck a match underneath her, she sat up straight in bed.

"Absame," she said, at first in a barely audible whisper.

"What?" Jake asked confused.

"Absame!" She yelled, repeating his name over and over as tears streamed uncontrollably down her cheeks. "No, I didn't betray you! I wouldn't! Please!" She cried. Jake protectively put his arms around her and tried to calm her, to remind her that she was safe. He called for the nurse and requested a sedative to help Kat sleep.

Once he was sure that she was resting peacefully, Jake quickly wrote down what he was able to make out about Kat's outburst. He sat with her for another hours or so, until it was time to meet the others for breakfast. He couldn't wait to see what the others would make of this new piece to the puzzle.

The house seemed so empty with half the team still in New Orleans. Ryan was the last one to come in and sit down once breakfast had been served. Jake told them about Kat's spontaneous memory.

"You are sure about this name?" Ryan asked looking at the piece of paper Jake had given him.

"Yes, sir. She kept repeating it over and over. Do you know who this is?"

"Possibly. Let me get back to you." He immediately got up and left the room.

As the meal was coming to an end, Reese and Sarah returned to the compound. Ryan welcomed them back.

"I hope you didn't have too much fun on your little holiday," Ryan teased. Sarah grimaced and they all enjoyed a laugh.

"I need to take a long shower after spending the weekend with such despicable people," Sarah shuddered. Reese was quick to agree.

"Well you both did a great job of blending in," Ryan complimented.

"Sir, what do we know about Gabriella?"

"Not much, I'll have the techs do some more digging. Do you suspect something?"

"It's more a feeling than anything else."

"Well, I'll see what we can find out."

"Thank you sir."

Jako came out to the training field later that day and told them that one of the detainees had committed suicide over the weekend. Apparently, he would rather die than give up any information.

"I guess that tells us what kind of monsters we're after," Jake said.

"I've had a few run-ins with the Somalians, and they really are quite barbaric," Jako commented.

"Well, I think I'm gonna go for a swim and clear my head," Reese announced to the group. Sarah, BJ, and Janie decided to join him. Jake decided to head up for a shower, then he would go down to see Kat. Her outburst had really bothered him. It made him realize that she may still be in some serious danger, and he knew that it would take everything he had to keep her safe. No one should have to experience the things that she had, and he would make sure that she would never have to experience them again. Jake thought about how he had never cared this much about anyone before, let alone a total stranger.

Kat had just finished her dinner by the time Jake made it downstairs—if you could call broth and red Jell-O 'dinner'. Kat noticed his grimace and knew what he was thinking. She smiled at his scowl. If was the first actual emotion he had seen on her face, and it changed every single one of her features. Without commenting on it, Jake just sat down beside her and asked if she felt up to a game of chess. They spent the next two hours in competitive play.

Jake could see that she was getting tired, so he called the nurse in to administer her meds. He sat with her until she was finally able to drift off. Just as he was getting up to leave, Sarah appeared in the doorway.

"Jake you look tired. Try to get some rest. I'll sit with her. She won't be alone. And you aren't alone in this either.

"Thanks Sarah," he said, placing a hand on her should as he glanced back at Kat one last time. "I'll see you in the morning."

Sarah sat in the chair that Jake had just vacated and opened a book. She ended up just watching Kat sleep for a few minutes, in awe of what a remarkable woman she was. A few hours later, Sarah had dozed off in her chair; her book still lying face up in her lap. Suddenly, Kat sat up screaming in terror. Sarah jumped back into consciousness and tried to calm her.

"Kat, it's okay. You're safe. It's okay!" But the woman was frantic. Sarah ran to the door and yelled for the nurse. Kat needed a mild sedative to get her to calm down enough to find sleep again. Just then, Janie came down.

"Hey, what's going on in here?"

"I don't know; she just woke up screaming. We couldn't get her to calm down without the sedative," Sarah explained.

"Well, why don't you go up and get some rest. I'll stay with her the rest of the night."

"Thanks Janie."

Chapter Sixteen

Reese and Jake were the first to arrive for breakfast and were having light conversation when Sarah and BJ joined them. Janie came in just a few minutes later.

"Hey, how is she?" Sarah asked as soon as Janie sat down.

"They had to sedate her again just a few minutes ago."

"What happened?" Jake asked alarmed.

"She's been having nightmares all night where she just wakes up in a total panic, screaming. We can't get her to calm down without the sedative. It's like she's locked in a part of her brain that she can't get out of," Sarah said sadly.

Jako came in and announced that Ryan would be joining them after lunch today, and he was bringing with him a new assignment. The group assumed that it was probably in connection with Mendoza. Jake told them that he would catch up with them on the run; he wanted to go down and check on Kat first.

The group decided to add an additional five miles to this morning's run. Once they returned to the compound, sweaty and exhausted, most of the team went upstairs to shower. Jake wanted to peek in on Kat first. She had been asleep when he went down the first time. He was glad to see her awake when he walked into her room, but he could tell that she wasn't rested.

"Hey you," he said softly.

"Hey."

"Do you want to talk about it?"

"I don't really remember anything."

"That's okay. If you do remember something, you can always tell me. Even if you don't think it makes sense. I'm here for you."

"I know. You've all been so good to me. Ah, I wish I could remember!"

"It's okay. Don't put so much pressure on yourself. Whatever is locked up in there is obviously pretty terrifying. It'll come out when you're ready."

"I hope so."

"Trust me."

"I do…I mean… I know that I can…for some reason. I know that sounds crazy. After what I just experienced, I shouldn't trust anyone ever again," she half laughed.

"It doesn't sound crazy. Listen, I gotta go shower up, but I'll be back later okay?" She only nodded in response. He turned to leave, and as he reached the doorway, she called out to him. He turned back around to face her.

"Thank you," she was only able to meet his eyes briefly before she looked down at her fidgety fingers. She peeked up through her eye lashes at him. He just smiled at her and tapped the door frame twice before leaving. Jake found himself smiling all the way back to his room.

Ryan joined the crew toward the end of lunch.

"When you're all finished here, please join me in command. By the way, how's are patient doing?"

"She's been suffering from some horrible nightmares," Sarah told him.

"But she says she still can't remember anything," Jake added.

"Her case manager is getting harder to keep at bay."

"I don't think she's ready for that kind of a push yet," said Jake. Ryan agreed, but he would have to have an official conversation with the doctor.

Kat was awake when Ryan entered her room. She was healing nicely. He almost didn't recognize her from what she looked like the first night they brought her in. They chatted for about twenty minutes before he had to excuse himself for his meeting upstairs.

As soon as everyone was seated, one of the techs put the briefing up on the flat screen.

"This man is Cabaas Cadiid. We believe he is in business with Mendoza. While being high up in the food chain, we don't think he holds a position of real power. Our intel says that he's got orders to take a Turkish freighter on its way to Galveston Port—right in our backyard, so to speak. We are calculating the attack to take place in three days' time. We really need to take this one alive ladies and gentleman."

Ryan transferred Vice President Woods into the meeting and delivered the update.

"The CIA is itching to get their hands on her, sir, but we all agree that she just isn't ready yet for that kind of mental and emotional push," said Ryan.

"Agreed. You have my approval to tell them to cool their jets. I'll setup some roadblocks for them here in DC," said the Vice President.

"Thank you sir."

If was after two o'clock by the time they made their way out of command. Half of the team went to the study to map out a plan for the operation, while the other half went to prepare the weapons and diving gear. They analyzed Cadiid's photo so that they knew every freckle on their new target's face. One thing was for sure, the fact that they would have to take him alive made the mission all the more challenging.

Chapter Seventeen

Jake went up to dress for dinner a little early; he wanted to get some time in with Kat. By the time he made it down to her room, Ryan was just leaving.

"Hey Buddy, I'll see you upstairs," Ryan said, clapping him on the back. Kat was sitting up in bed. She was gaining her strength back a little more every day, and Jake was pleased to see that. Kat just watched him as he moved across the room and sat down in his usual spot. She hadn't seen him so dressed up before. *He really is very handsome*, she mused. *In a rugged, Black Ops kind of way…just my type*, she chuckled to herself. *Hmmm, I didn't know I had a type.* Jake just sat and watched the variety of thoughts dance through her head.

"You look nice," she said finally, realizing that he was just sitting there watching her while she let her thoughts run away with her.

"What's going on in there?" he said, tapping his index finger to his temple.

"Oh…" she blushed, "nothing. Nothing, I thought I remember something, but I'm sure it's nothing."

"Do you want to talk about it?"

"No, no it's nothing really," she cleared her throat uncomfortably. "So, where you headed all dressed up like that?"

"Dinner is being served in the formal hall tonight. It helps us practice being rich and sophisticated before a new mission." They laughed together. "Mind if I come back later for a game of chess?"

"Please do."

"It won't be much longer before you can join us upstairs for these fancy dinners. I can feel it."

"I sure hope you're right." They shared a smile before he turned and left. The hospital staff came in shortly after with Kat's dinner. She immediately turned her nose up at it. *This is for your own good*, she told herself. *Just pretend it's a ribeye, a touch on the rare side. Hmmm, that's another new one. I didn't know I liked red meat, let alone a little rare*, she pondered as she sipped her broth. After she ate, she pushed the tray aside and tried to nap before Jake returned.

Sarah came down the stairs and found Jake already in the dining room.

"Hey, how's she doing tonight?" she asked.

"She seems to be in good spirits—getting stronger. You can see it in her eyes."

"Good! I'll come down to relieve you around two if that's alright."

"Sure. Thanks Sarah." He poured them both a drink and the two made small talk until the others joined. Half way through their meal, a call came through on Reese's undercover line. It was Mendoza requesting a meeting for the next day at his club in New Orleans. Ryan suspected that it had something to do with the freighter. Then, the conversation turned back to Kat.

"Don't you think it's a bit strange that the CIA is trying so hard to strong arm their way to Kat?" Jake asked the group as a whole. "I mean…think about it. She's been missing for months. Why are they all of a sudden so worried about her?"

"The CIA doesn't exactly honor the same code as you all. Not leaving a man or woman behind doesn't really apply to them. They thought that she was dead, so they wrote her off as a loss to the mission. Now that they know she's alive, that means their mission is still alive and they are itching to know what she knows," Ryan explained.

"That is wrong on so many levels," Reese commented. "This girl must present a serious threat to somebody." They all agreed. "So, we protect her until she can shed some light on the whole operation."

"And then we keep protecting her, as far as I'm concerned. She's one of us now, and we aren't going to leave her behind," Jake added passionately. Again, they all agreed. They split up and went their separate ways after dinner. Ryan headed to command to have a call with the Vice President. Professionalism aside, he had to smile when he spoke of what a perfect team they had assembled. Jake went back down to see Kat for that game of chess he promised. When he got there, Kat was ready and waiting with the board already set up. He laughed at the competitive mischief in her eyes as he sat down. He let her win the first game; the next she won all on her own. He could tell that she was getting tired, so he put the board away and helped her get comfortable for the night. She was fast asleep in two minutes flat. He made himself comfortable in that old chair and watched her sleep until he felt himself beginning to doze. As he drifted off into sleep of his own, his last thoughts contemplated that possibility that he may actually be falling in love with this girl.

He was awakened by the sound of Kat thrashing around in her bed. Still asleep, she was actually trying to get out of the bed. He gently put pressure on her shoulders and eased her back onto her pillow. Before he knew what happened, or how it happened, he felt the softness of her lips pressed against his. Jake was brought back to his senses by the sound of footsteps coming down the hall. He quickly straightened and pulled the covers back over Kat's, now resting, body. Sarah entered the room and smiled at Jake tucking Kat in. Without a word, Jake nodded his greeting to Sarah and left the room.

Sarah shook her head as she sat down. She felt bad for Jake. She knew him to be a loner, but she also knew that you didn't always have a say in who you fall in love with. Speaking of love, Sarah found her thoughts wandering over in Reese's direction. She lived by the rule that you should never date a coworker, but she had never worked so closely with such an interesting man before. If they didn't have each other, they didn't have anyone.

Janie came down before breakfast to check on Sarah and Kat. Sarah informed her that Kat had slept peacefully through the night. The two women made their way upstairs to eat and get ready for the meeting with Mendoza. Being around Mendoza was by far Sarah's least favorite part about this mission. He just made her skin crawl without even trying. Jake, on the other hand, was looking forward to going into town today. He figured it was best to put a little distance between himself and Kat, so that he could get his thoughts in order.

The techs fitted them with watches and a necklace with hidden cameras and audio. Their ear wicks were also undetectable. Soon, the limo was waiting out front. They would need to get an early start if they wanted to beat the Mardi Gras traffic. Once again, Jake and Janie would act as bodyguards to the couple.

The streets were packed with party-goers. Once they finally made it to the club, Mendoza's thugs were waiting for them out front—reserving them a parking spot. Sarah thought this shady strip club was the perfect place for nefarious meetings. She took Reese's hand as Janie and Jake followed behind at a safe distance. As before, Mendoza was holding court at a table in the very back. The club itself was packed, but Mendoza kicked everyone out as soon as they arrived—just like last time. As always, his manners were impeccable; though he still tended to hold Sarah's hand for just a few seconds too long. It was all she could do not to cringe when he pressed his vile lips to the top of her hand. Her acting skills were really being pushed to the limit.

Reese stuck his hand out, encouraging Mendoza to release Sarah's. They shook cordially, and Mendoza invited them to sit down. He ordered them drinks without even asking what they wanted. He was not used to people telling him what to do. At least there wasn't any coke on the table this time. Reese was learning that Mendoza did not like to get right down to business; he liked to play the big shot for a while and strut around a little bit first.

Two men joined the table a few minutes later. Reese and Sarah immediately recognized one of them as Cadiid. Mendoza politely made all of the necessary introductions. Mendoza and Cadiid spoke in Spanish to one another for a moment before Mendoza turned to Reese.

"Apologies my friends, but something has come up. Can we meet again in a week? I think you will like what I will propose."

"My time is just as valuable as yours," Reese countered. Mendoza's mask of manners slipped a little and Reese could see the shadows in his eyes. But, he quickly recovered.

"Yes, of course, my friend. Unfortunately, this cannot wait. I will call. I will take you and your lovely wife out to make up for the inconvenience— somewhere very special."

Sarah and Reese took their leave, suspicious as to what was happening. As soon as they were safely in the limo, Ryan's voice could be heard booming through their ear pieces.

"What the hell do you think you're doing Reese? What part of making him angry do you think is beneficial for this mission? We'll talk about this when you get back."

Chapter Eighteen

Mendoza watched them leave. That was the first time in a long time that someone had dared to speak out against him. He found it somewhat refreshing…somewhat. Cadiid filled him in on the plans to take the freighter. He asked about the Americans. He was suspicious of them.

"They are not your concern."

"Absame will not like this, my friend," Cadiid warned.

"What happens in America or Mexico doesn't concern our relationship at all." Cadiid didn't like this response at all, but he held his tongue. He would be reporting back to Absame later.

Jake drove the limo back to the compound. BJ stayed behind to follow Cadiid and his men. They stopped at the townhouse in town to wait for BJ to call. Jako told them that going back to the townhouse would look better for their cover anyway in case they were being watched. It would also give Ryan some time to cool down.

It was a good thing they had decided to stay in town, because Mendoza showed up an hour later.

"My friends, I am so sorry to interrupt your evening. I just didn't like the way our meeting ended. Please join me for dinner. Emeril has cleared a reservation for us. I know how much your beautiful Sarah enjoyed it there last time. Our reservation is at eight. I will see you there."

Ryan was on the com-system and gave them the green light.

"Stay the night. We will keep an eye on Cadiid from here." They all went upstairs to prepare for the evening.

As before, there were men outside the restaurant waiting for them to arrive. They were escorted directly to the table. Janie stood to the right of Sarah where she had a clear view of the patrons, and Jake watched the back of the restaurant—Mendoza's men behind him. They earned a few looks from the other patrons—probably trying to figure out if they were celebrities. If they knew the truth, most of them would probably leave.

Mendoza apologized again for having to cut their meeting short earlier. Reese graciously accepted the apology. Mendoza requested that Reese deliver two hundred additional guns with ammo.

"Not a problem at all," Reese told him, "But I can't guarantee the same pricing as last time."

"If it was," Mendoza laughed, "I would think you were up to something."

"Glad we understand each other," Reese said before taking a sip of his beverage. Once dinner and dessert had been served, Mendoza asked if they would like to join him for the parade. They agreed politely.

By the time they made it back to the townhouse, Jake and Janie filled them in on what they had witnessed. For a moment, they thought that the pirates were going to make their move that night. Ryan radioed in and told them to get some sleep, then get back to the compound first thing in the morning.

Janie and Sarah went upstairs to bed. Reese, BJ, and Jake went into the living room for a night cap and a smoke; Mendoza had given them a box of Cuban cigars as a way of making amends.

"If I didn't know what a rotten guy Mendoza is, I could probably be friends with the bastard," Reese admitted. Jake and BJ agreed—except for those few seconds when he let his friendly mask slip; then the dangerous side of him really came through. Shortly after, BJ called it a night, while Reese and Jake decided to have another drink.

Meanwhile, Thomas was still on the stakeout watching Cadiid. He saw a pair of headlights approaching. Mendoza got out of the car as Cadiid walked over to greet him.

"Absame isn't happy about your new American friends," Cadiid told him.

"I don't really give a damn what he thinks," Mendoza countered. "He will come around when he sees the deal that I am working for his new arsenal."

"I really don't think you can count on that changing his mind."

"Let me worry about that. Are we all set for tomorrow tonight?"

"Yes, everything is in place." Mendoza took his leave. As soon as he was out of sight, Cadiid got on the phone and ordered whoever he was talking to to keep watch on the American's townhouse. Thomas quickly sent an alert to Reese and Ryan.

"You need to clear out fast!" Ryan barked. "Tell the servants to pretend that you live there and that you are just out for a various number of reasons…at least for the next day." Reese woke the others and they hurried out the door. Leaving the limo behind, Ryan sent them to the helo pad where Janie was able to fly them back to the compound.

Chapter Nineteen

Back at the base, Kat was having another violent nightmare. Jako was with her at the time and held her down as he yelled for a nurse. Jake entered just as the sedation was taking effect.

"Thanks Jako. I'll stay with her." Jake sat down beside her and took her limp hand. "I'm so sorry I wasn't here when you needed me," he told her. He could only hope that she heard him.

Sarah made her way down to the hospital ward three hours later.

"You should take a break."

"I'm fine," he insisted. She gave him a sad look. "I just want to be here when she wakes up." She nodded in acknowledgment and let the room.

The team gathered for a late breakfast and decided to run through their plans for the operation again. Ryan advised that they not overdo it on this one. He knew that they were under a lot of pressure and insisted that they take the afternoon off to rest.

Janie was headed down to visit Kat. She was awake when Janie entered the room. Janie thought she saw a split second of disappointment run through her eyes.

"Just me," Janie said smiling.

"Sorry, I was expecting Jake."

"I know. He'll be down soon. He is just running maneuvers with the rest of the team."

"New mission?"

"Yep."

"I wish I could get out of this bed. I'm so sick of sitting still. I feel like I should be out doing something."

"Care for a game of chess?"

"Absolutely!" Kat agreed, eager for anything that would challenge her mind. They were already in the middle of their second game when Jake came in.

"I should get going. Thanks for a great game. I'll come back and say goodbye before we head out," Janie promised. She left and made her way back to the command center to find Ryan.

"I want to give Kat an ear wick," she said to Ryan. He only stared at her in response. "She was showing sincere interest in this mission. I think being able to hear what's going on might trigger some memories for her." After thinking it over for a moment, Ryan agreed.

Janie headed back down to Kat's room, feeling very pleased with herself. Jake gave her a strange look. As she explained her plan, Kat lit up. Jake wasn't thrilled with the idea, but Kat certainly was.

"I don't know how to thank you enough," Kat said hugging Janie. Janie smiled hugging her back, then went upstairs to get ready.

"What's eating you?" Kat asked at the sight of Jake's grumpy face. He cracked a smile despite his best efforts. He was so handsome when he smiled. "I'll be fine," she assured, assuming the answer to her own question. "I need this…I need to feel like I'm a part of something." He smiled again and squeezed her hand, then went to get ready for the mission. He ran into Ryan on his way up.

"Please make sure someone is with her at all times. We have no idea what kind of crap this is gonna stir up for her."

"Don't worry Jake. I won't leave her side, Ryan promised. Inwardly, Ryan hoped that he would not regret this decision. Ryan had received word again from the CIA, pressing him for access to Kat. He lied and told them that she was still in a coma, and that he would contact them when something changed.

Kat had fallen asleep while she was waiting on the team to arrive at the appropriate location. She suddenly awoke in a cold sweat and sat straight up in bed. Ryan in sitting in the chair beside her.

"Kat, you were calling the name 'Carl' in your sleep. Do you know who that is?" Ryan asked.

"No Sir."

"He was your handler for the undercover CIA mission you were working when you went missing. But, it seemed as though you were almost afraid of him in your sleep. Do you remember anything about him?"

"No sir, I'm sorry." Just then, they received word that the Ops team was ready to begin. Kat was so excited to be a part of the excitement in this way.

Everything was playing out exactly as they had planned. Until suddenly, Janie noticed a pirate coming up from behind Jake. Shots were fired. As Jake fell to avoid the shower of bullets, he was able to return a few shots back at the target. Just as he was taking cover, he saw Janie go down. All was quiet for a moment; Jake had successfully taken out his target. Kat and Ryan held their breath as they listened to the sounds of Jake rushing to Janie's side.

"Get her off the freighter now!" Reese ordered. Sarah and Reese gathered the rest of the men. BJ and Thomas restrained Cadiid and returned with him to the yacht. Janie had taken a bullet in the lower part of her abdomen, just below the vest. Ryan had already called for a rescue chopper to come in. In the meantime, Jake and BJ field dressed the wound and gave her morphine for the pain. Only fifteen minutes had passed by the time the chopper arrived. The medics immediately got her stabilized and loaded her into the chopper. Sarah flew back with her. The pirate who had shot her didn't survive. BJ and Thomas took the freighter to a secluded cove they had discovered; a crew would be sent to pick it up later. They took the tobacco boat and headed for the compound.

Chapter Twenty

Ryan, Jako and the medical staff were standing by when the chopper arrived. Janie had not regained consciousness. The medics rushed her down to the hospital ward. The doctor met them at the double doors and instructed the nurse to take her straight in for surgery. Kat watched all this from her hospital bed. All of the excitement was causing her to have flashbacks about her own experience being shot.

The team gathered in command. Ryan assured them that there was absolutely nothing they could have done differently. Janie had followed her training, and she was getting the best possible care. Ryan asked Jake and Reese to join him in interrogating Cadiid, then suddenly thought better of it. It would be better not to broadcast their real identities, just in case Cadiid was able to get word to the outside. Ryan would do the interview alone.

Jake requested that he be allowed to go check on Kat. Ryan gave him the okay. She was still awake when he entered the room.

"How is she?" Kat asked the second she saw him.

"She's still in surgery. I don't know much else," he said sitting down. "How are you feeling? Ryan said you enjoyed being a part of the operation, in a sense."

"Yes, it felt so familiar to me for some reason."

"Have you been able to remember anything else?"

"Just flashes here and there," she paused for a moment. "I'm really glad you made it back safely."

"So am I," he smiled. "Can I interest you in a game of chess?"

"You certainly can." She laughed, swinging her bedside table into position. "But what I would really like to do is get out of this room. I can't even remember the last time I took a breath of fresh air."

"You know what...I'll be right back." He returned a few minutes later with a wheelchair.

"Are you serious?" She asked as Jake lifted her from the chair and into the chair.

"I just got the okay from the doctor." The nurse adjusted her IV and Jake wheeled her through the house and into the courtyard. Kat closed her eyes and took a deep breath, smiling to herself. She felt more at peace now than she had in months. She wished she could sit out here all day.

"We have a formal garden too. Are you up for a short ride?"

"Absolutely!"

Ryan and Jako were waiting for Janie to come out of surgery. They were told that it had been touch and go, but they should be able to visit her in a few hours. It wasn't long before the entire team had filtered into the waiting room. Jake made sure that Kat was still feeling up to it. She assured him that she wanted to be there when Janie came out and promised to tell him if she started to get tired.

Chapter Twenty-One

Mendoza was just sitting down to breakfast. His newest woman, Jenna, sat across from him with a black eye and a busted lip. One of his men brought in a cell phone, announcing that Absame was on the line. Mendoza put the phone to his ear, and Absame launched into a half-English rant.

"Whoa, whoa, calm down Absame." Mendoza was silent for a moment as he listened. Suddenly, he hung up the phone and through it across the room, narrowly missing Jenna. Mendoza yelled for his man to come back and told him that the freighter had been taken and that all of their men were either dead or captured.

"I want the people responsible for this, and I want them dead!" he fumed.

"Si Senior." His man went out into the courtyard and began shouting orders to the rest of Mendoza's crew. Mendoza went straight to the liquor cabinet and poured himself a stiff drink. He threw back the drink in one gulp and poured another. He hated losing money, and more than that, he hated his business partner, Absame. Absame was becoming a liability and a pain in his ass. It would be hard to get rid of him, but Mendoza knew that he would find a way. He poured himself a third drink and went upstairs to find Jenna. The men preparing the weapons in the courtyard didn't pay any attention to her tortured screams.

Meanwhile, back at the compound, the doctor was just walking into the waiting room.

"She's not out of the woods yet, but the next twenty-four hours will tell us a lot about her chances for recovery," the doctor announced.

"Thank you doctor," Ryan said before turning to the team. "Why don't you all go up for a late dinner. I'll stay and hang out with Janie and Kat for a little while." Jake started to argue, but Kat insisted that he go get something to eat.

"I'll be back in a few hours," Jake said more to her than to anyone else. Kat just smiled and they all headed up to the dining room. Shortly after, the nurses wheeled Janie into the room, and laid her to rest in the bed next to Kat. After such a long day, Kat welcomed sleep with open arms. Ryan settled into the recliner in the corner room and kept watch over the two women.

Kat woke with a start a few hours later. By this time, Jake had taken Ryan's place in the recliner.

"Are you okay? What's going on?" Jake asked concerned.

"I remembered something. Something about Carl Radford, but now I can't pinpoint exactly what it was."

"Okay, I'll bring it up to Ryan and Jako anyway."

"I just wish I could get my mind to focus. I know it's important."

"You're doing great; a little better every day. Don't pressure yourself like that. Try and get some more rest. I'll be right here when you wake up." Jake assured her. Sarah was standing near the doorway. She waited until Kat had dozed off again before she entered the room.

"Has there been any change in Janie's progress?" Sarah whispered.

"Not yet," Jake frowned.

Ryan and Jako were getting nowhere with Cadiid. He wasn't going to tell them anything and would be sent off to Guantanamo the next day. He was under constant surveillance. They didn't want to give him any opportunity to commit suicide.

Chapter Twenty-Two

The next morning, Jake poured himself a cup of coffee and grabbed a bagel before heading down to see if Kat and Janie were awake. Ryan caught him just as he was walking out and asked him to sit down for a minute.

"We have reason to believe that Carl Radford had something to do with Kat's cover being blown. The vice president and I have decided to bring him in to see what kind of response it triggers in Kat. Of course, we have already gotten the okay from the doctor."

"She mentioned something about him last night. She couldn't remember what exactly, but she brought up his name and sensed that it was something important. Can I be present when you bring him in?" Jake asked.

"Of course. We really don't want to upset her, but if the man is dirty, we need to know about it. He may even be on Absame or Mendoza's payroll." Ryan explained. Jake nodded in acknowledgement. The rest of the team came into the room for breakfast, and Jake excused himself to the hospital ward to relieve Sarah. Sarah told him that there had still been no change with Janie and that Kat had slept soundly the rest of the night. Jake sat down and let his thoughts wander as he waited for Kat to wake up. He couldn't help but think that he would kill Radford if he did turn out to be involved somehow in Kat's injuries.

Just then, Kat began to stir. Her eyes fluttered open and focused on his. She turned her head to see Janie still resting next to her.

"How's she doing?" she asked.

"No improvement yet, but she's tough…like you."

Back upstairs, Ryan was filling the others in on their plan for Carl Radford. "BJ and Thomas, I want you two to go up to DC and bring Radford down here. He is not to know where he is going, understand?"

"When do you want us to go?"

"As soon as possible," Ryan answered.

"I'll have the jet standing by in thirty."

"Kidnapping him might be our best option here. But remember, he's a spook, so you will have to be careful."

"Leave him to us sir."

BJ went down to the hospital ward to let Jake know that he and Thomas were preparing to go retrieve Radford. As he was about to leave, Janie began to stir. Jake rushed to her side and took her hand. As soon as she was able to focus on his face, she asked what happened. Jake helped her remember their last mission and told her that she had taken a bullet in her lower abdomen.

"I'm so sorry you were shot, Janie, but it is kind of nice not to be the only invalid in this place," Kat said, trying to lighten the mood. Janie laughed, but had to stop herself as she discovered that she was still in a lot of pain. Jake called for the doctor to let him know that she was awake. He came in to check both women and administer their pain medication. They were both soon resting peacefully. Jake left them and returned upstairs.

Sarah came down a little while later to check on Kat and Janie, but they were both still asleep, so she decided to head out to the shooting range. It was a soothing kind of therapy for her to shoot her guns and clean them. Reese was standing watching her. When she finally turned around and noticed him, she asked if he wanted to join her. They spent an hour in compatible silence—only the sound the shots singing out into the air.

It was time to gather for dinner. Sarah was leaving her room and about to head down the stairs when Reese called out to her.

"Hold up a second. I'll walk with you," he said locking his door. Ryan and Jako were standing at the bottom of the stairs deep in conversation. BJ and Thomas weren't back yet. Jake found everyone in the dining room and filled them in on Janie and Kat's progress. After dinner, Sarah excused herself up to her rooms. She wanted to catch up on some reading. Reese decided that he wanted to enjoy this beautiful night and went for a walk. Ryan and Jako were scheduled to have a call with the Vice President. Jake, of course, resumed his place in the hospital ward with Janie and Kat. Shawn and Bill made their way to command to analyze some new intel from the techs.

Mendoza stood waiting patiently for Absame to arrive. There were no leads as to who could have attacked their men on the freighter. Mendoza had been so angry, that he shot the messenger carrying the bad news on the spot. Absame showed up right on time. He was practically foaming at the mouth.

"Someone is targeting our operation. I want them caught…now! And if you don't think you can handle that, I will," Absame barked. Mendoza struggled to maintain is temper. He would have loved to put a bullet in this arrogant man's head. But, for now, he still needed the bastard alive. The second that changed, Mendoza swore to send him to hell where he belonged.

Chapter Twenty-Three

BJ and Thomas had followed Radford for two days, observing his behavior. They would make their move tonight. They set up a false road block and shot his bodyguards with tranquilizer darts. After knocking out Radford, they handcuffed him, and left the car and bodyguards in the middle of the road. They packed up the cones and barricades and made their way back to the jet. BJ called Ryan to let him know that they had been successful and were on their way back.

Ryan and Jako smiled to each other. Reports of the kidnapping would be all over the news by morning. Ryan almost wished that he would be there to watch it all unfold in person. Jake was talking to Janie back in the hospital ward. Kat was away having some x-rays taken. Ryan came in and informed them that BJ and Thomas were on their way back with Radford and that the chopper should be landing by midnight.

"We will bring him down to see Kat in the morning. I want him to sweat a little more tonight," Ryan told them. "BJ says he hasn't stopped blubbering since he woke up. I told him to just knock him back out." They laughed.

A few minutes after midnight, Ryan got the call that Radford had been safely secured in the dungeon—their affectionate name the makeshift jail below the compound. When Ryan made his way down, He found Carl sitting in a cell, still handcuffed with a hood over his face. Ryan decided that he should stay that way until he came face to face with Kat. So, Carl sat trembling in fear the remainder of the night.

Jake went down to relieve Sarah in the hospital around four that morning. Both Janie and Kat were resting peacefully. So, Jake settled into the recliner and allowed himself to fall back to sleep. The sun coming through the window woke Jake a few hours later. He was surprised to see that Kat was already awake and smiling at him.

"Hey. Why didn't you wake me?" he asked with sleep still in his voice.

"You look so sweet when you're sleeping," she answered playfully. Just then, Ryan came in and let Jake know that it was time. Then, he turned to Kat.

"There is a man here to see you from the CIA. Jake, your doctor, and I will be in the room with you the entire time, okay?"

"Are you feeling up to this?" Jake asked.

"Yes," she answered confidently. The doctor came in and Jake pulled his chair closer to Kat's bed. BJ and Thomas brought Radford in and removed his blindfold. Kat immediately gasped and put a hand over her mouth. Carl's eyes focused darkly on her for a moment, and he instantly knew that she remembered everything. However, the look passed quickly, and he opted for the role of concerned colleague and mentor. But, the whole room had already seen the truth written all over his face. He began to move towards Kat, but Jake and Ryan formed a barrier between them.

"What is the meaning of this?" Carl began, "She's my agent! And I'm taking her home." Thomas and BJ came up behind Carl and each grabbed an arm to restrain him. They took him out of the room as Jake and Ryan sat down with Kat.

"You can't do this to me! I am a federal agent. I will have all of your heads for this!" Carl yelled as he was drug down the hall.

"Did you recognize him?" Ryan asked.

"Yes. He's working with Absame. He basically sold me to that bastard Mendoza. I don't know what exactly was negotiated in the trade, but he blew my cover to protect his own ass and fill his pockets. I almost died because of him! I can't believe I trusted him!" Her eyes welled up with angry tears.

"You're safe now, and we are going to do everything we can to make sure he is punished for the rest of his life," Jake promised.

"What's going to happen to him?" Kat asked.

"We're planning to send him to Cuba with the others, unless Vice President Woods has other plans for him," Ryan answered. Kat's blood pressure had skyrocketed because of the encounter. The doctor ordered that she be left alone to rest for the next couple hours.

Ryan and Jake went down to Carl's cell. The man was stilling ranting about making sure none of them had jobs by the time he was finished with them. Without a word, Ryan walked into the cell and slammed his fist into Carl's jaw.

"After what you did to Kat, you're lucky I don't let my friend Jake here have you all to himself for the next hour," Ryan growled. "What was it that made you turn Carl? The CIA doesn't pay as well as you hoped?"

"I don't know what she told you, but she's lying. It's all lies!"

"The woman can barely remember what she had for breakfast and you're accusing her of lying? Yeah, that should go over well in front of a jury. Try convincing your firing squad of that one," Ryan laughed as he watched the color draining from Carl's face.

"I still have rights! I want out of here now!" Carl demanded.

"That's not going to happen. You, my friend, are on your way to a secured location, and thanks to my agents, the world thinks you disappeared without a trace. By the time we're done with you, you'll never be in a position to betray your country ever again. I can promise you that."

"Release me now damnit!" Carl screamed repeatedly as the cell door slammed behind Ryan. Both Ryan and Jake chuckled a bit as they listened to his screams all the way back up the stairs.

Chapter Twenty-Four

Absame paced the floor, waiting not-so-patiently for news on Radford. Amiin entered a few minutes later to report that there was still no sign of him.

"The CIA is looking for him too, so it's safe to say that he didn't suddenly switch teams."

"Do you still have access to the grandchild?"

"Yes, Absame."

"Keep looking for him, and have our CIA contact find out more. What the hell am I paying him for!"

"It will be done Absame."

"Amiin, make sure we can get the child. I have a feeling we will need her." Amiin bowed in response and left the room. His thoughts turned to what would happen to the child. Hurting women and children was something that he had never grown used to, but he would do what was required of him. He didn't have a choice; it was their life or his.

Back at the compound, Kat asked the nurse to call Jake and Ryan for her. As soon as they entered the room, she told them that she wanted to talk to Carl.

"I don't think it's a good idea Kat," Ryan hesitated.

"Please...I need to see him again."

"Alright, I'll have him brought up."

"No, I want to see him where he is being held," she requested. Jake had started to argue, but Ryan agreed.

"Maybe he will talk to her. All we're getting is threats," Ryan reasoned. Jake went to go get the wheelchair. When they made it to the stairwell, Jake picked Kat up and Bill came from behind to carry the chair down. Kat shivered as they made their way deeper into the dungeon. She was having flashbacks of being held in a place just like this. They could still hear Carl making a ruckus as they approached, but he grew quiet as soon as he noticed Kat.

"Can we have a few minutes to ourselves please?" Kat asked Jake, Bill, and Ryan. Jake refused, but Ryan ordered him out of the room. "How could you do this to me?" Kat asked as soon as they were alone.

"Kat, I wish I could explain. It was one of the hardest things I have ever had to do. I had no choice." Kat just stared at him.

"I remember a time when you once said that we always have a choice. It's just a matter of making the right one, especially in our line of work. So tell me, Carl, because I need to know, what made you think that betraying me and committing treason against our country was the right choice?"

Carl took a deep breath. "My granddaughter. They said that if I didn't give them the information they were looking for, they would kill my entire family, starting with Laya. They had an entire file of surveillance photos of my family. They were watching every move they made and could have killed them all at any moment."

"So you gave me up because I was the most expendable."

"Yes, and I have regretted it every single day Kat. If I don't get in contact with them right away, they are going to start killing my family," he said sobbing. Kat just stared at him for a moment.

"I loved you like a father. You were the closest to one I've ever had. You made me a part of your family, and then threw me away. I hope you rot in hell Carl." She wheeled herself to the bottom of the staircase and yelled for Jake to come get her.

She was quiet all the way back to her bed. The men respected her need to grieve. Janie was having x-rays done, so after Ryan and Bill returned to command, Jake and Kat had the room to themselves. Kat finally allowed herself to meet his eyes and saw the sympathy in them.

"I can only imagine how you are feeling right now," he said softly. "But just know that we are your family now, and we won't abandon you...ever." Kat smiled at him as the tears returned to her eyes. He took her in his arms and held her until she couldn't cry anymore.

"I honestly don't care what happens to him, but isn't there something that can be done about his family? They shouldn't have to pay for his sins."

"Protecting the innocent is what we do. I'm sure Ryan already has plans in place to make sure that they stay safe." His reassurance made her smile. Janie was rolled back in just a moment later and both women were told to rest. Jake promised to check in on them later.

After leaving the room, Jake went straight to the command center and wasn't surprised to see the rest of the team already there. As suspected, they were already formulating a plan to get Radford's family into protective custody.

"We're going in blind on this one guys. We can't say for sure whether we'll encounter Mendoza's men or Absame's, but either way, we can count on the situation to be extremely dangerous."

"I think I speak for everyone when I say that we are more than willing to take on this assignment, regardless of how dangerous it might be," Reese said. They all enthusiastically agreed.

"Count me in too," a familiar voice said from behind them. They all turned and were shocked to see Janie standing in the doorway. Actually getting a clear read from the x-rays, the doctor had released her.

"Are you sure you are feeling up to this?" Ryan pressed.

"Wouldn't miss it for the world boss," she replied.

"Alright, start with the grandchild. She is going to be the one they go after first. Intel tells us that she is living in Baltimore with her parents. They would need to be rescued first, followed by Mrs. Radford. You'll have to work fast. Shawn, I will need you to escort Radford to Guantanamo, and then go to meet up with the team ASAP."

"Yes, sir."

Reese, Sarah, and Jake went over the intel as new information came in. They knew that they needed to perform to the best of their ability if the girl was to live; neither men had any qualms about killing women or children.

Chapter Twenty-Five

Mendoza was having breakfast with Jenna when Cruz came in to let him know that there still hadn't been any sign of Radford or their missing men. He checked with every source they had, and no one knew anything.

Meanwhile, Absame had just finished questioning his other mole in the CIA. Again, coming up with nothing. Absame became so enraged that he instantly slit the man's throat.

"Amiin, find me another source," he demanded.

Back at the compound, Kat was frustrated to be left behind again. But, she could still only stand and walk for short distances. Ryan promised that he would bring her up to command when the time was right. As she waited, she began to remember the day Radford had recruited her. Having been in-and-out of foster homes all her life, she finally just ran away and worked odd jobs here and there to pay her own way. Carl approached her and offered her what sounded like an incredible career opportunity, with travel and paid training included. She jumped at the chance; that had been ten years ago.

Kat was happy to realize that she was getting more and more of her memories back—most of which included Carl and his family. She hoped that, this time, she belonged to something truly good, something real.

The team headed out to the runway and boarded the plane. Janie was glad to be back in action. She sat down in the cockpit and smiled, feeling truly at home. Thomas took the co-pilot's chair and they prepared for take-off.

Jenna was finally able to make it out of bed after the latest beating. She didn't understand why Mendoza had been so angry all the time, but she knew she wouldn't be able to take much more of his attacks. There wasn't a place on her body that didn't hurt. She knew that she desperately needed help. She couldn't put her finger on why, but something about the kindness in Sarah's eyes when they met at dinner the other night made Jenna feel like she could trust her—like maybe she could even have a friend in her. Jenna checked the house and found that there was only one guard standing at the bottom of the stairs. She climbed into her closet and called Reece's phone number as it was listed in the phone.

Sarah answered the undercover line. She could barely make out Jenna's frantic words. Sarah was able to calm her down and promised to help her if she could; she just needed to sit tight for a little while longer. Jenna promised to try. She memorized

Sarah's number then deleted all record of the call. She felt like she finally had a life line.

Back at the compound, Kat had just awakened from a dream about Jake. In the dream, he was a real knight in shining armor—well, a knight in tarnished armor. The kiss he had left on her forehead was such a small thing, but she knew that it meant a lot coming from such a stoic man.

Kat had always stayed away from romance because of her career. She wasn't sure if she was even capable of real love; she hadn't even really thought about it before. Ryan came in just then and asked her if she was ready to head up to the command center. She couldn't wait! Her hospital room seemed so empty without Jake, Sarah, and Janie to keep her company.

A few minutes after getting settled in command, they heard Reese's voice come over the sound system, informing them that he, Thomas, and Sarah were in place and ready to retrieve Mrs. Radford. Jake radioed in only seconds later saying this his team—Bill, BJ, and Janie—were also in place at the child's home.

"Any resistance at your location?" Reese asked Jake.

"We're counting five men hanging out outside the house. I am sure they are armed, but they are still being subtle."

"There's two parked at my location," Reese informed.

"Alright men, let's move…God be with you all," Ryan ordered. No sooner had the words left his lips that the sound of gunfire rang through the speakers. Ryan, Jako, and Kat sat quietly and waited anxiously for a report of any kind, but all that seemed to keep coming was more and more gunfire. Then, there was an eerie silence—which seemed even more frightening to Kat than the gunfire had been.

"Location clear. All family members secure. We're safe," the sound of Jake's voice caused everyone to release the breath they didn't even realize they were holding.

"Location clear here too. Mrs. Radford is safe," Reese's voice followed. The command center broke out into cheers and applause.

"Alright crew, the police are en route; move out," Ryan said.

"Hey boss, one of the men at my location got away, but I made sure he was injured," Jake told him.

"Copy that. See you when you get back. Good work team." Kat breathed a sigh of relief. Jako asked Kat if she was ready to head back to her room. She nodded in acknowledgment. Jako was quiet on the short walk to the hospital ward. He knew that her thoughts were with the Radford family.

"Get some rest Kat. We'll be sure to wake you when everyone gets back."

"Thank you Jako."

Chapter Twenty-Six

Six hours later, Absame was just rising when Amiin was carried in. Absame yelled for the other men to get a doctor in there. Amiin was barely conscious and was rambling incoherent words. Absame was trying to calm him so that he could understand what he was trying to say, but wasn't successful. He was still mumbling nonsense when the doctor arrived. The doctor spent hours treating Amiin and said that the next forty-eight hours would be crucial. Absame had his men show the doctor out, then made his way to Amiin's bedside. He spoke to him even though he wasn't being heard.

"I've always been able to count on you, my brother, but you have let me down." Absame then turned and walked out of the room.

At the compound, the team gathered to deliver their reports. They were all pleased to see Kat sitting at the table with them.

"Who do you think it was that got away?" Ryan asked Jake.

"I suspect it was one of Absame's men. The one who was calling the shots. I know I hit him at least three times."

"What makes you think these men belong to Absame?"

"The fallen were all Somalian."

"Simon, get Vice President Woods on the line please," Ryan ordered. Ten minutes later, they were joined by the Vice President via video cam.

"My men have been able to conceal most of the mission," Woods told them. "We've been able to blame it on a gang rivalry in the area. Very good work ladies and gentlemen."

"Thank you sir," they all answered in unison. Once the Vice President was off the line, Sarah told them about the call she had received from Jenna.

"Okay, we will work on getting her out. This could be the opportunity we need to blow Mendoza's men apart too," Ryan said. "Do you think she will have any intel?"

"I'm not sure, but I'm willing to bet that a man like Mendoza brags about his way to the top quite a bit. She's had to have overheard something," Sarah answered.

"I hope you're right. We could really use something solid. Alright everyone, get some rest. Great work tonight. We will meet in the morning and go over our options."

Jake pushed Kat back to her room. "I missed you," she admitted out of the blue. Before he could even recover from the shock, he heard the words 'I missed you too' falling out of his own mouth.

"Soon you will be able to join in on the fun," he told her.

"I can't wait!"

"As soon as the doctor gives you the okay, I'll take you out to the shooting range. I'm willing to bet you've gotten a little rusty," he teased.

"Hey!" she said, playfully swatting at him. Sarah watched their flirting silently from the doorway, smiling to herself before slipping away unnoticed. She knew what they were feeling— mainly because she was feeling it too. She knew that she shouldn't have feelings for someone she lived and worked so closely with, but Reese had gotten under her skin before she could even decide what to do about it. She had started up the stairs to her room when Ryan called out to her.

"They are setting up dinner a little early tonight, so that you can all get to bed at a decent hour. Will you let the others know?"

"No problem." She passed Reese in the hallway and asked him to relay the message to the men; she would let Janie know. Ryan had already requested clearance from Kat's doctor that she be allowed to have a real meal. He agreed as long as

Ryan promised not to let her get too tired. Janie and Kat ravaged their closets and were able to put together the perfect evening attire for Kat; they didn't want her to feel out of place and uncomfortable in her hospital gown. They finished getting ready, then went down to help Kat get dressed. They did her hair and makeup and truly helped her to feel like a woman again—something she rarely did even when she was healthy.

Jake walked in to push her up to the dining room. He stopped dead in his tracks and just stared as if he had never seen a woman before. He told her how beautiful she looked and the four of them made their way to the study where everyone else was waiting, cocktails in hand. Jake poured Kat a glass of white wine. The conversation was light and the mood in the room was warm. Shortly thereafter, they were called in for dinner.

Ryan had pulled out all the stops for them. The waiters were in tuxedos, and all of the dinnerware was crystal. They started with shrimp cocktails, followed by turtle soup, and a Caesar salad. They enjoyed a main course of lobster tails and fillet mignon with red potatoes in a butter sauce and corn on the cob with a Cajun spice rub. It was all Kat could do not to shovel everything into her mouth at once after two months of nothing but broth and Jell-O.

"Take it easy kid; you're gonna make yourself sick," Jake warned, only half joking. He hoped she would actually be able to keep it all down. Kat was sure she wouldn't be able to hold another bite; that is, until they rolled the Banana Fosters cart in. Sarah saw the look on Kat's face and assured her that it would be the best thing she had ever tasted in her life.

After dinner, they all went out on the terrace to enjoy a glass of cognac while the men smoked Cuban cigars. As much as Kat hated to admit it, she was really getting tired. She finally broke down and asked Jake to take her back to her room. Sarah and Janie offered to go instead so that they could help her change back into her hospital gown. Not ten minutes after being helped into bed, Kat was sound asleep.

Chapter Twenty-Seven

The next morning, Jake went down to check on Kat early, but found that she was still fast asleep. He asked the doctor if he could bring her down some breakfast.

"Since she handled dinner so well last night, she can eat whatever she wants now, as far as I'm concerned," the doctor answered. Jake excitedly took off up the stairs, silently kicking himself for acting like a giddy, love-sick puppy. Janie was just entering the dining room when Jake jet passed her with a plate full of food. When Jake returned to Kat's room, she was awake and sitting up in bed. She stopped brushing her hair for a second as she noticed the tray of food. Then, a huge smile played across her lips.

"Is all that for me?" Jake just returned her smile and swung the bedside table around in front of her. Her eyes bulged when he lifted the lid. "Oh my god, are you guys trying to fatten me up!"

"Don't worry, I thought we could share," he laughed. "What would you like?"

"All of it!" They ate together laughing and talking about the fun they'd had at dinner the previous night. "I can't believe the difference in my energy level since I'm able to eat real food now."

"Do you want to go out to the gardens for a little while?"

"Absolutely." Just then the doctor came in and said that he would have to run some tests. Jake picked up her tray and promised to be back later. The rest of the team was just finishing up their breakfast when Ryan came in and asked them all to join him in the command center.

"We've just received word about another heist being planned. Taking the freighter and Carl's disappearance has greatly angered two of the largest pirate parties in the world. I'm positive that they have already recruited a new mole in the CIA, most likely Homeland and the FBI as well. This could very well be a setup, so it is imperative that you remain in deep Black Ops. Reese, I need you, Sarah, Janie, Jake, and BJ to spend a few days in town. Sarah, see if you can make contact with Jenna. Shawn, Bill, and Thomas, I need you three to go back to Guantanamo and see if you can get anything out of Carl. Tell him that we were able to get his family out alive. Also, I want you to lean on Cadiid."

"Yes sir!"

The team arrived in the city later that afternoon and set out to be seen in all the right places. Hopefully, Mendoza would make contact first. Reese and Sarah slowly made their way down Bourbon Street, stopping at several shops along the way. Janie and Jake played 'bodyguard' behind them.

In Cuba, Bill, Shawn, and Thomas had landed and were making their way to the special holding cells. They checked in on Carl first. The man looked like he had aged ten years in the few days he had been there. Bill let him know that his family was safe, so now he owed them a written statement of his activity with Absame and whether or not he had any involvement with Mendoza as well. Carl insisted that the only ones he had ever dealt with were Absame and Cadiid. Next, they made their way to Cadiid's cell. Bill and Thomas spent several hours trying to crack Cadiid, but he wasn't talking. Shawn told the guard not to let up on Cadiid until he was ready to start talking. The men returned to Carl's cell to retrieve his official statement. They thanked him and made their way back to the plane. They had just boarded when they suddenly realized that the pen was missing. They ran at top speed back to Carl's cell, but they were too late. Carl had stabbed himself in the jugular with the pen and the bleeding couldn't be stopped.

At that same moment, the guard from Cadiid's cell came running over. Apparently, Cadiid had bashed his own head in against the cell wall.

Bill ordered that both men be buried at dusk, then called Ryan. Ryan ordered them back to the compound as soon as possible because he needed to get to Washington. He put Jako in charge of command in the meantime.

A short while later, Jake and Reese called to let command know that Mendoza had just made contact. He wanted to welcome them back into town by inviting them to dinner at his mansion that evening.

Promptly at eight o'clock, Reese, Sarah, Janie, and Jake arrived at Mendoza's residence. Mendoza greeted them at the door personally, greeting them as if they were the best of friends. His men did their usual pat down.

"My friends, I would like to introduce you to my business partner, Absame."

"Oh, I didn't realize this was a business dinner," Reese said taking Absame's hand, but looking at Mendoza.

"Nonsense, there will be no business at dinner," Mendoza replied, waving off Reese's comment as if it were an annoying nat. They had finished their first course when Jenna joined them. Sarah immediately noticed the fading bruises all over her body. She meekly apologized for being late. Reese held out her chair for her. Mendoza didn't seem pleased by the gesture, but made no comment. Absame hadn't taken his eyes off of Sarah since the second she walked through the door. Jake and Janie were both highly aware of the man's acute attention to their friend. Reese sat back down and the meal continued with small talk around the table. After the last course, Mendoza told Jenna to show the women to the patio. The all stood as she led them out of the room.

Mendoza requested that his servants bring bourbon and cigars to the men. "Reese," Mendoza began, "my good friend Absame and I have a business proposal that we feel you might be interested in."

"I'm listening," Reese replied.

"I've decided to take you up on another shipment of rifles and ammo, if you can get me twice the amount."

"That shouldn't be a problem…for double the money."

"Of course, my friend," Mendoza answered.

"May I ask what your interest in this deal is?" Reese asked Absame.

"I just want to make sure my partner is not making a mistake by trusting an American," Absame answered honestly.

"Well we've already been doing business together so I don't think he gives a damn whether or not you think he's making a mistake," Reese said standing up. Absame shot to his feet as well.

"Gentleman," Mendoza interrupted. "Please, have a seat." With the distraction in place, Jake planted a bug in the room. "We are all business men here. There is no need for bad blood my friends. Let us drink and enjoy these fine cigars." Reese and Absame sat back down, but refused to break eye contact. Mendoza ordered one of his men to retrieve the women. The men stood as the ladies reentered the room. The conversation lightened, and Mendoza invited them to another gala he was throwing in two weeks' time.

"Would it be alright if I took Jenna shopping for the occasion?" Sarah asked sweetly. Mendoza looked from one woman to the other for a moment.

"No problem," he finally agreed. Reese laughed out loud.

"Classic mistake my friend," Reese chuckled. "You did not ask where they will do this shopping."

"Paris of course," Sarah smiled and looped her arm through Jenna's. Jenna stared at Mendoza in shock as he answered.

"Sure, why not."

"But, I will only be able to spare a few days my love," Reese told Sarah.

"Let them go, my friend," Mendoza said, "They will have the bodyguards."

"Very well. I will make the necessary arrangements."

"Nonsense, I will be sure that everything is taken care of," Mendoza insisted. The remainder of the evening was actually pleasant. When it was finally time to leave, Jake motioned for everyone to keep quiet until they made it back to the townhouse. Jako continued listening through the bug that Jake had planted in Mendoza's dining room.

"I came here to talk about our missing shipments, my missing people, not to socialize with American pigs!" Absame spat.

"Calm down. The money we will make off of those weapons will take away from of the loss from those shipments. The quality of his product is hard to come by."

"Why not just kill him and his filthy wife and take the product?"

"Because this man is an asset, and I like him."

"Mendoza, you don't like anyone. You just want his wife."

"Maybe you should think about getting yourself a new woman It's been months." Absame didn't reply to his comment, but if looks could kill, Mendoza would be dead ten times over.

"What are we going to do about this unknown enemy?"

"My men are looking into it. Still no sign of Cadiid?"

"No, he's been with me since childhood. If it weren't for him bringing in Carl Redford, I would have never known about Kaitlyn."

"Your mistake was not killing her when you had the chance," Mendoza said. "Trying to sell her was stupid and risky."

"You worry about your affairs, and I'll worry about mine."

"I would, but your affairs have brought us trouble, and I don't like trouble. Find these people and kill them."

"Don't threaten me Mendoza," Absame growled before storming out of the house.

Chapter Twenty-Eight

Jenna lay awake long after Mendoza had left the room. She had to get away from him, but she was terrified of the man. She really didn't like getting Sarah involved either, but the woman truly seemed to care about her which was something she hadn't felt in a long time.

Sarah awoke before Reese and headed downstairs. Jake was already up having a cup of coffee. He poured her a cup and asked how she was holding up. It was safe to talk in this room; it was the only one that Mendoza hadn't bugged. They had also found two in the limo and more on the jet.

"Are you worried about the trip to Paris?"

"No, I'll have you and Janie with me."

"What made you pick Paris?"

"Well, with all the unrest that's been going on over there, anything can happen."

"Good thinking. Man, that Absame radiates pure evil, doesn't he? It was all I could do not to just kill him on sight, but he deserves a slow death, not a merciful one."

"Agreed," Sarah said, taking a sip of her coffee. Just then, Reese made his way down the stairs. Janie was right behind him.

"So what's the plan for today?"

"Whatever we do, we want to keep visible," Reese answered.

"I would love to go back to that sidewalk café with the amazing eggs benedict." So, they would start there. They got dressed and had BJ bring the car out front.

Mendoza called around three o'clock and requested that Reese meet him at the club...alone. Janie and Sarah went about their shopping and Jake accompanied Reese to Bourbon Street. Mendoza was there with Absame; they were able to come to a final agreement on the weapons and ammo.

"Thank you gentleman. I will be back in touch as soon as I return to New York," Reese said. They agreed on a meeting place. It didn't take long for Jake to realize that they had picked up another tail.

Back at the compound, Kat couldn't believe what was happening to her. For the first time in a long time, she had woken up and knew exactly what she was. It was as if everything had just magically come back to her overnight. No more struggling to put bits and pieces together. The doctor told her that she could now begin physical therapy to start building up her stamina. She wished that Jake was there, but he wouldn't be back for at least another day, and then there was the trip to Paris after that. Jako came down to check on her.

"How's the team?" she asked.

"Everything is set in motion," he smiled. "I heard about your physical therapy. It will be great to see you up and walking."

"It's going to feel great!"

Reese and Sarah were enjoying a quiet dinner on Bourbon Street. Janie and Jake stood by as guards. They truly appeared to be a normal, everyday, rich, newly-wedded couple in love. Reese asked if Sarah would be interested in a walk on the river. Of course, she was. Jake and Janie had spotted three people following them. They knew two of them were Mendoza's, and assumed that the other belonged to Absame. They received a report that the freighter had set sail a few hours ago. Ryan and the techs hadn't been able to get a tracker on it, and it was too risky to have anyone follow on open water.

After their walk, the couple decided to call it a night. As they stood waiting for the limo to pull up, they noticed Mendoza and Jenna approaching.

"What a pleasant surprise, my friends! You are not calling it a night so soon are you?" Mendoza said.

"We are. We were just looking for a quiet night out and that is exactly what we got," Reese answered.

"Would you care to join us for a night cap?" Mendoza asked. Reese hesitantly agreed. They walked together toward a pub called O'Malley's. Even on a week night, the place was packed. Reese and Mendoza enjoyed a glass of Crown Royale X, while Sarah and Jenna ordered their world famous Hurricanes. The group ordered one more round before they sent for their cars. Mendoza asked that Reese meet him at the club for brunch the next morning. They shook hands and went their separate ways for the night.

Once the team was safely inside the townhouse, they delivered their report to command, then called it a night. Sarah was awakened by a strange noise. By the time she was fully awake, she realized that Reese already had his gun out. Janie came crashing through the door and got the man to the ground. Apparently, he had come through the window. Reese and Jake went to check the rest of the grounds and found one more man. A third had run off through the back gates, but the alleyway was empty now.

Reese reported the break-in to command, then finished searching the house to make sure that nothing was missing. Jake was just getting ready to call the police and turn the men over, when there was a knock at the door. Jake answered and recognized Mendoza's men. Reese joined Jake at the door.

"We apologize for the late hour Senior. We were ordered to watch Absame's men. We have the one that ran, if you could release the others to us." Reese and Jake exchanged looks. Reese finally agreed, and they brought the men forward. Mendoza's man thanked them and led the two captives away. The team decided to sleep in shifts so that one person was on guard for the rest of the night. Jake took first watch. He rechecked all of the windows on the first floor and toured the outside grounds as well. He rechecked the front and back gates. He was suspicious of the man who had come to the door. Jake had recognized him as one of the men who had been following them since the beginning.

Chapter Twenty-Nine

Ryan had Radford's body brought to DC. They put it in a wrecked vehicle and set it on fire, to make his death look like an accident. This way, his wife could receive his pension. The arms deal would take place in ten days. The team would need to regroup at the compound to go over the next phase of the mission. Ryan would meet them back at the compound in two days. He had another meeting with the Vice President. He had worked alongside the Vice President for a long time, but this was the first time he was given Black Ops authority and the free reign to use it. Vice President Woods believed that what they were accomplishing here was perhaps the most instrumental strike there would ever be on terrorism.

Ryan sat down in his empty DC apartment and found himself missing the bustle of the compound, the activity of the team, and the chaos of the command center. The way they all took care of each other showed just how much of a family they had become. Suddenly, a knock at the door interrupted his thoughts. He put a hand to his gun as we approached the door, not expecting any guests.

"What the…" he said under his breath as he checked the peep hole. He opened the door and came face to face with Carly Hatch. She was an old flame of his, but also a CIA agent.

"You look surprised to see me. Can't an old friend stop by to say hi?"

"Of course, but…how did you know that I was in town?"

"You must not have heard about my promotion."

"No."

"I'm the new assistant director of in-country relations. So, that means I'll be in town a lot. I'm not sure what good that will do me though, because it seems like you are out of town even more. Anything I should know about?"

"Why does my travel itinerary mean anything to you?"

"Oh, you know how rumors fly in this town. I know that Carl Radford was hounding you about a missing agent."

"Carly, you know better than to go around asking questions like that."

"Are you going to invite me in? I could sure use a drink."

"Alright, but just one. I have an early meeting at the White House."

"Looks like we're both moving up in the world."

Carly left three hours later. He knew it was a bad idea, but if he had refused, she would have started digging around where she shouldn't, and that could end both of their careers. Ryan was ready to get back to the compound. *Home*, he thought, not knowing exactly where the thought came from. Ryan looked at his watch. At least he could get a few hours of sleep.

Carly was determined to find out what Ryan was hiding. He wasn't usually so evasive, especially in bed.

Back at the compound, Jake and the team had just landed on the helo pad. Shawn picked them up and told them that Ryan was due back in a couple of hours. Sarah said that she was headed to her room for a while. It was good to be back home where she didn't feel like she was constantly being watched. Janie went up with her. Reese and the others went to command to check in with Jako. They gave him a brief on what happened while they were in New Orleans. Jako told them to get settled and that Ryan would call them all together when he got back.

Before heading up to shower, Jake went down to visit Kat. He turned the corner and was shocked to see her up walking around the hallway. He felt a surge of pride as he watched her. Her eyes met his and it was as if they were the only two in the room. Her therapist cleared his throat and asked Kat if she was ready to call it a day. She nodded, her eyes not leaving Jake's. Jake followed them back to her room

"How did the mission go? From what I heard, things went well," Kat said once the therapist was gone.

"It went well. From the looks of things, it won't be long before you are out there with us." They sat and talked for the longest time; Jake filling her in on all the details she had missed. Sarah came down and told them that Ryan was back and wanted everyone in the dining room in five minutes. Sarah told Kat that she looked great.

"Yeah and you should have seen her cruising up and down the hall a little while ago," Jake announced proudly.

"Wow! Good for you!"

They made their way upstairs. Ryan stood quietly as his team assembled before him. It felt so good to be back. He filled them in on everything that had happened in DC—minus his meeting with Carly.

"I want you all to rest up the next few days. We will have to be on our A game if we are going to finish out this mission strong. Sarah, Janie, and Jake will be leaving for Paris, and Reese, Thomas, and BJ will return to New York. I need the rest of you hear to monitor and translate new intel. The shipment is ready to go. It was a little tricky getting all of those guns, especially knowing where they were going, but we knew it was necessary for this to work. We have plans to track them and get them back before they fall into the wrong hands."

Chapter Thirty

Absame was back in New York. His men had secured a new mole in the CIA and he was due to meet with her the next day in Washington. Absame didn't trust women—especially spies. Kaitlin had found her way through all of his defenses. It still made him angry to remember how much he had loved her. After he found out that she worked for the CIA, he beat her for days. She never broke, so he sent her away. The fact that she could possibly be alive after what he and his men had done was a miracle.

The last time he spoke to Radford, he knew that she was alive, but still in a coma that they weren't sure she was going to wake from. If she were still alive, it wouldn't be for long. He was not one to let betrayal go unpunished. If Cadiid ever made it back, he would also feel Absame's wrath.

Absame called in his guard and told him to procure a whore with blonde hair and green eyes. Amiin walked in the room a moment later. Absame smiled.

"You are back from the dead my friend."

"Yes Absame. You seem angry."

"You know I don't like to lose, Amiin. Are you able to travel?"

"Yes, where do you want me to go?"

"Washington to meet my new informant. Leave me now. I'll be down shortly," Absame said as the guard returned with a woman. Amiin bowed and left the room. Amiin was surprised that Absame had not ordered him dead. He would have to do whatever it took to make sure that he did not fail again. Amiin left the penthouse; he couldn't stand the sound of the screams coming from Absame's room. The guards kept their posts outside the door, seemingly unaffected. Once in the lobby, he made all of the necessary travel arrangement to Washington.

Back in New Orleans, Mendoza was also preparing to travel. He would be leaving for New York, as well as sending Jenna off to Paris. He almost wished he could go with the women. Sarah fascinated him. He knew she couldn't stand him and that only made him want her more. One of Mendoza's men came in, interrupting his thoughts.

"Juan, you are to make sure the women come to no harm. I don't trust the Englishman. If something happens to the lovely Sarah, don't come back."

"Si Senior Mendoza. I will protect her with my life."

"Good. Send Jenna in please." Jenna cringed when Juan told her that Mendoza had requested her, but she made her way to his side.

"I want you to have fun on this trip. And try not to turn Sarah against me even more. Do you understand?"

"Yes, of course. I would never disobey you."

"Good girl. Go pack."

Jenna was shaking as she walked away. The look in his eyes when he talked about Sarah made her blood run cold; it made her think that if he ever got his hands on her, Sarah would have it a lot worse than she got. Jenna was starting to feel guilty about putting Sarah in harm's way just to save herself. But, what other option did she have? She knew that her next beating from him could be her last.

Chapter Thirty-One

The team was already at breakfast when Kat walked in with only a little help from her physical therapist. Jake immediately stood up and pulled out her chair for her. Ryan started to clap and soon everyone joined in, completely embarrassing Kat.

"I wouldn't even be here to be able to do this if it weren't for you all. What you have given me, money could never buy," Kat told them graciously.

"Welcome to the family," Sarah replied. Ryan lifted his cup in cheers with all the others. After breakfast, the team split up—half went for a run and the others went into the training yard. Jake asked Kat if she would like to head down to the shooting range. She was really excited about the idea. Kat chose a nine millimeter glock, as did Jake. They spent an hour working on target practice. Jake assumed that Kat would be a little rusty, but she was dead on, hitting the bullseye almost every time. Ryan and Jako were watching from the gate, impressed by her accuracy.

"She'll be back in the field in no time," Jako said.

Once the others had returned from their run, they all got cleaned up and sat down for an early lunch. After lunch, Kat was eager to get back to her room. She was exhausted and even felt like she needed a bit of pain medication. Jake told her to get some rest and assured her that he would be back before dinner.

Janie and Sarah were in command going over their plans for Paris. Jake, BJ, and Reese joined them. Once they felt like they had everything mapped out, they presented it to Ryan.

"Good work team. This will be hard to beat. Listen up everyone," Ryan called out as Jako was wheeling Kat in. "Dinner is going to be a special event tonight. Our dear Kat here, has graduated to a room upstairs with the rest of you. She has officially been released from hospital care. Kat, Sarah and Janie did a little shopping for you, so please go on up and make yourself at home."

Kat was shocked by the splendor of the room. She walked to the closet and let her fingers trail each beautiful garment inside. She heard a knock at the door and opened it to find Sarah, Janie, and a young woman Kat had never seen before. Sarah introduced the woman as their maid who would be helping Kat get ready for dinner tonight.

Ryan, Jake, and Reese stood at the bottom of the stairs chatting as the three women descended.

"Close your mouths gentlemen," Ryan teased under his breath. Ryan offered Janie his arm. Jake and Reese followed suite. Kat didn't know if it was the food, the wine, or just the company, but this night felt magical. She hated to see the final course come and go. Ryan was the first to excuse himself after dinner, as he said he needed to make a phone call. From the look on his face, Kat thought it might be something important. Jake asked if she wanted to go for a walk on the beach. She politely asked for a rain check. He bid her goodnight and she returned to her new room. Jake went to the study with the others for a drink. After having her maid help her into a silk night gown—a vast improvement from the hospital gowns she was living in—Kat made her way out to her private terrace. It truly was a beautiful night, and the way the moon shone on the ocean was magnificent. She was beginning to regret not taking Jake up on his offer. She went back inside and sat down on the bed. She noticed a prescription bottle sitting on her side table. It said: "Take 1-2 tablets every 4-6 hours as needed." She took out one tablet, then another. *This may be worse than any of my injuries,* she thought to herself as she swallowed the medication. *Oh well…*

Jake was surprised when he didn't see Kat sitting at the breakfast table the next morning. He tried knocking on her door, but there was no answer. Reese told him that the three women had gone out a little over a half hour ago. Jake sat down at the table with his plate trying not to seem concerned. Reese almost felt sorry for him.

"I think they just went for a workout," Reese said encouragingly. Jake didn't respond; he just finished his breakfast and left the room. BJ and Reese couldn't help but bust out laughing at their comrade's expense. Jake checked the gun range first—not there. He found them in the gym. Kat and Janie were in the ring. He stood and watched from the doorway. Ryan and Jako found them a few minutes later.

"It really is amazing how quickly she is bouncing back. She'll be ready for a field mission soon," Jako said.

"It's just going to get harder and harder to hold her back," Ryan added. After working in the ring for a little while longer, the women went to the shooting range. Reese and Jake opted to go for a run. Thomas, Shawn, and BJ were preparing the weapons for their next operation. It took about another hour for Kat to finally throw in the towel. Sarah was amazed that she had even lasted that long. The woman had an iron will.

"Lunch will be ready soon girls," Jake said as he approached. "Don't you think it's time to call it?" The girls laughed, but agreed. Kat went up and ran herself a hot bath. It felt like every bone in her body was aching. She stopped by the nightstand and took two pills before going in for her nice warm soak. Once she was dressed and ready, she popped two more pills before heading downstairs to join the others.

"There she is," Ryan said as she entered the room. "Hey Kat, the doctor would like to see you once you're finished with lunch." They sat, talked, and laughed as old friends do. After lunch, Kat went down that familiar hospital corridor for her check-up exam.

"How has your pain been Kat? Any trouble sleeping?"

"I have been having some pain, but I have also been really active the last couple of days. I had to take an extra dose of the pain meds after my workout this morning."

"I will order you a Phentanol patch that will work in conjunction with the pain medication. That might help bring you some added relief. I'll also prescribe you some Ambien to help ensure that you are resting soundly."

"Great, thank you doctor." Jake was waiting for her at the end of the hall.

"So…good news?" he asked when she came out of the doctor's office. "He told you to quit over-doing it didn't he?"

"Of course he did," Kat laughed.

"And are you gonna listen?"

"Only about as well as you would in my place."

"Touché," he laughed. "Well, anyway, the real reason why I'll here is because Ryan wants to know if you are feeling up to a trip into town. They want to see if you recognize the men that have been following us."

"What if they recognize me?"

"Come with me Kat; there is something that you need to see."

Ryan was sitting at his desk in is private office when Jake and Kat entered.

"I think she's ready to see the file," he told Ryan. Kat sat down in the chair across from Ryan and opened the file that he handed to her. It was her service file from the CIA. Kat stared at the picture.

"I don't understand… that's me. So…" she looked up at the mirrored wall behind Ryan's desk. She stood up slowly and got closer to the mirror as she took in her reflection. "My god…" was all she could bring herself to say.

"When we first brought you here, the damage was so severe that we couldn't even begin to identify who you were. The doctors worked miracles, but they had no idea what you looked like before. So, you get to start completely over," Ryan explained gently. Kat took a deep breath and turned her back to the mirror.

"I would love to go to New Orleans with you," she said smiling. She couldn't even begin to explain why this revelation felt so freeing, but it did. She had a fresh slate in every essence of the word.

The team decided to head into town the next day. The regular team took the limo, while Ryan, Jako, and Kat arrived by helicopter with a black Escalade waiting for them. Reese and his team would follow routine of making themselves know, while the rest would wait and watch. It wasn't long before Mendoza's men took notice of the team. Ryan held back and watched the Somalians fall in line. Kat was observing through a pair of binoculars.

"The man in charge is called Fowsi," she whispered. "It translates to 'success'. Absame sends him because he never fails."

"Never say never," Ryan replied.

"The other man, his name is Galmaan. These guys don't usually leave Absame's side."

"Good work Kat."

"Is there any way that we can walk by them?"

"Of course. You and Jako can walk over to that café over there. I'll watch and see if they take notice," Ryan said. "Be careful kiddo." Kat took Jako's arm and they made their way over to the sidewalk café. They sat down at a table across from Reese and Sarah. Ryan whispered into her earpiece that they men didn't even look twice at her. She smiled.

Reese's phone rang just then; it was Mendoza.

"My friend, I thought you would still be in New York."

"We left something behind at the house that Sarah apparently couldn't live without; you know how women are," he said lowering his voice into the voice. Sarah smirked at him from across the table. "We'll be flying out later."

"Come to the club," Mendoza told him. Reese didn't think it sounded like much of a request. Ryan came and picked up Kat and Jako, then went back to the chopper. Reese and Sarah arrived at Mendoza's club about an hour later. Mendoza met them at the door; the club was completely empty. "Well, my friends, all is set for the day after tomorrow."

"Good, I'll be ready."

"Are you ready for your shopping spree?" Mendoza asked, turning to Sarah.

"I am always ready to shop in Paris," she replied with a smile.

"My men have orders to protect you at all costs, my dear."

"I'm sure you mean Jenna too."

"Of course, my dear," Mendoza laughed. "Reese, my friend, my I have a private word?"

"Sure. Sarah, why don't you meet me back at the house. Jake and Janie will accompany you. BJ can just come back and get me after he drops you off."

"Janie can go. I'm staying here," Jake said with authority.

"It's not necessary Jake, please take Sarah safely back to the house." Reese insisted.

"Nonsense, nothing to worry about my friends. I will just send my car when we are finished here," Mendoza offered. Janie went with Sarah, and Jake stayed with Reese.

Back at the command center, Ryan wasn't happy with this turn of events. He didn't like his people being outnumbered by Mendoza and his men. But, as it turned out, Mendoza only wanted to ask Reese for his opinion on Absame.

"I don't really have an opinion of him. The only thing that was clear to me was that he obviously didn't care much for me or my wife," Reese answered.

"His culture doesn't care much for women in general."

"Can we have this discussion again once our deal is complete? I will have more to go on then, as far as Absame is concerned."

"Good answer my friend. I won't keep you any longer. I will see you in New York. Give the lovely Sarah my well wishes." The men shook hands and Reese left the room without another word. There was a car waiting for him at the curb. Reese and Jake rode in silence back to the townhouse. Reese could tell by the look on Jake's face that he wasn't pleased with the way the meeting had gone.

Chapter Thirty-Two

Back and the compound, Jako and Ryan were not pleased either. They instructed the group to get back as soon as possible so they could discuss everything further. After the team had boarded the plane, Jake and Reese got into a heated discussion about how Reese went all cowboy on them. Sarah suggested that they wait and discuss everything out in the open back in command. The rest of the flight was in total silence.

Mendoza was preparing to leave for the airport as well, when he got a call from Absame.

"Everything is ready for the deal. If all goes well with this American, then we will bring him in," Absame said. The look on Mendoza's face after the call was enough to make even the bravest of men cringe. Jenna was watching from the staircase and thanked God that she would soon be out of this life.

When the team arrived, Ryan asked Reese to join him in the study. He told the others to go on in to dinner. Jake shook his head and led the way into the dining room. It was a very quiet dinner. Ryan and Reese were still locked in the study by the time they were finished. Everyone went upstairs except for Sarah.

"Reese, you were chosen because of your leadership skills. I knew you were a bit of a cowboy, but so far you've managed to play pretty nice. So much could have gone wrong," Ryan lectured.

"Yes, it could have when Jake didn't follow orders."

"A good head of security doesn't leave his employer, Reese. You know that."

"Yes sir. It won't happen again."

"See that it doesn't. We are going into our most critical mission yet."

"Yes sir." Reese left the room, and Jako entered just a few seconds later.

"You heard?" Ryan asked.

"Yes, what do you think?"

"I think if the need arises, he'll do the same thing."

Reese was surprised to see Sarah waiting for him. "Well, you don't look any worse for wear," she said.

"You want a drink?" he replied.

"Sure." She waited as he poured. "Are you really upset with Jake?"

"No, he did exactly what he was supposed to do."

"If he hadn't then I would have refused to leave." Reese handed her a glass and they sat in silence.

Chapter Thirty-Three

Absame didn't like hotels, so he had a Brownstone in the city. Mendoza was staying at the Ritz Carleton in the penthouse. They were scheduled to meet later in the day. Reese and Sarah were due to show up early the next day. Mendoza left his clubhouse to check on things at the club and make final preparations for the exchange. He always got a rush before a big deal. He would celebrate with Jenna, but make sure that Sarah didn't see the aftermath. So, instead, he told Juan to bring the new dancer to his office.

In the command center, the team was getting last minute instructions. Kat was being incorporated into the mission. She would travel to New York with Jako and help monitor Absame and his men. She was fluent in their language and culture. Jake asked her if he could have a few minutes alone before they left. She agreed.

"What's up?" she asked.

"I just wanted to tell you to be careful and watch your back."

"I'll be fine. You're the one that's going to be in the line of fire." He took her in his arms and hugged her tight. She hugged him back, and they went back inside. They would fly to New York together, then Sarah and her team would change flights and head to Paris.

Jako and Kat arrived in New York on a separate plane. They would still be at the same hotel as the others. They were pretending to be an Irish business man and his young wife who was recovering from a car accident. They were on the same floor as Reese and Sarah. A tech team was already in place. Sarah and Reese were to meet Mendoza and Jenna in the hotel bar at six o'clock. Sarah, Jake, Janie, and BJ would fly out with Jenna and Mendoza's men early the next morning.

They had just arrived and Jake had already picked up on Absame's men following them. This was a good thing; they needed the men to follow them to Paris otherwise their plan could go up in flames. Ryan was also due to arrive the next day, but would not make contact directly with either team. His role was basically to make sure that local law enforcement didn't get in the way. Mendoza stood and offered Sarah his chair at the bar. He had already ordered them drinks, and told them that their table would be ready soon. Jake and Janie stood discreetly off to the side where they could survey the entire room. It was five minutes before the host came to take them to their table. Dinner was fabulous—as one would expect from a five-star restaurant at the Ritz Carleton.

After dinner and dessert, Sarah and Jenna excused themselves for the evening seeing as how they had such an early flight. Janie and Mendoza's men followed the two women to their rooms. Jake and Juan stayed with Reese and Mendoza. They were taken to a private room where they could smoke and have some Brandy. Jake and Juan swept the room briefly, and it came up clean. Jake turned on his watch recorder.

"We're live," Jako told Kat from their room. She reached for a set of headphones and put them on.

"So this will all be finished in forty-eight hours," Mendoza said to Reese.

"I thought tomorrow was the big day?" Reese asked.

"Absame says he needs another day." Reese got up and started to walk toward the door. "Please my friend. The man trusts no one."

"No one? Or just the American dealing you the biggest score you'll ever get?"

"Please, it's just one day."

"One day, if it doesn't happen, I will have another buyer ready."

"You have my word, my friend."

"Goodnight Mendoza." As Reese exited the room, Absame was just walking in. Reese didn't even acknowledge him.

"Well played gentlemen," Jako said into their earpieces.

The next morning, Sarah and Reese were having breakfast in their suite with Janie, BJ, and Jake when Mendoza knocked on their door. He had Jenna with him. He told them that the limo would be ready out front in an hour. Reese invited them to join for breakfast, but Mendoza insisted that they had some things to go over before they left.

"We will see you downstairs, my friends." Once they door was closed, they waited for the sound of the elevators before they spoke again.

"Jenna was looking mighty pale this morning," Janie commented.

"At least she doesn't have any fresh bruises," Sarah said.

"That's true," Janie agreed.

An hour later, they were all on their way to LaGuardia Airport so see the women off. Reese thought he recognized one of the security guards, but he couldn't quite place him. Before Sarah boarded, Reese kissed her goodbye and told Jake to take care of his wife.

"What are your plans today, my friend?" Mendoza asked as they watched the plane take off.

"I have some things to take care of before tomorrow, but I think I will try to relax the rest of the day."

"Shall we meet for dinner? Say around seven?"

"Of course." BJ followed close behind. It seemed they had picked up another tail.

Kat and Jako monitored both teams closely. Once Reese was alone, he asked them about the guard at the airport. Ryan confirmed that he was one of theirs.

"Okay good. I knew I had seen him before, I just couldn't pinpoint where."

"Is everything set for the exchange?"

"Yes sir, and everything seems to be falling into place in Paris as well."

"The guns are on a truck ready for transport. Every case has been fitted with a transmitter. ATF will be able to track and retrieve each and every one of them after Absame and Mendoza resell."

"All the plans for Jenna?"

"Good to go. It will look like Absame ordered it. Right now, all there is to do is wait. Get some rest team."

Kat didn't realize how much pain she was in until she returned to her room. She hadn't taken any pain medication that day. Going to the bedside table, she took two tablets and a sleep capsule with a double shot of Patron. She was soon sleeping soundly.

Chapter Thirty-Four

The girls landed at Charles de Gaulle Airport in Paris, France. Jake departed the plane first to make arrangements with customs. The other's followed ten minutes later. Jenna was absolutely mesmerized by the city. She even cried when the Eiffel Tower came into view. They would be staying at the hotel Brighton in the penthouse suite. Sarah told Jenna that they would be hitting Paris' best fashion outlets in the morning.

"First we'll go to Robert Clergerie to do a little shoe shopping, then to Bon Marche. That should put us just about at lunch time at Hotel Amour. We can plan the rest of the day out while we are eating," Sarah said excitedly. Juan gave Jake a pained look and they all laughed.

"Speaking of eating," Jake interrupted, "We have dinner reservations in an hour. Don't you ladies need to freshen up or something?" The women giggled and went to their separate rooms.

Kat listened in and wished that she were there with them. Just then, Jako told her that they had some new video of Absame that he wanted her to look at. She was grateful for the distraction. Absame was meeting with Mendoza; Reese hadn't been invited to this meeting.

Jake, Juan, and Janie dressed for dinner and waited for Sarah and Jenna to come out of their rooms. Two more of Mendoza's men and Thomas were also patrolling the hallway.

They enjoyed a fabulous dinner. Once they were finished, Sarah said she wanted to go for a walk down Rue des Barres. It was a beautiful evening. They stopped and watched as the Eiffel Tower lit up the night. It was truly breathtaking. They strolled for almost an hour before deciding to go back to the hotel. Jake and Juan made sure that the women were safely settled into their rooms before heading downstairs for a drink.

Once settled into bed, Sarah had time to be alone with her thoughts. She was worried about how thinly their team was stretched. She said a little prayer for a positive outcome for both of their missions and went to sleep.

Sarah was awake at first light. She might be living the pampered life of the rich and famous, but she couldn't shut off years of training and discipline. After the dinner she had indulged in last night, she thought she could certainly go for a run. She knew Jake would never go for it though. Sarah invited Jenna over to her suite and they called room service to have some breakfast sent up. The women talked about their plans for the day, and overall, spirits were high. Sarah sincerely hoped that Jenna would be able to follow through with the plan; she just seemed so fragile. Janie had repeatedly review the procedure with her and really tried to make her understand that this would be life or death for all of them. They weren't completely confident in her ability to not crack under the pressure—and that would both blow their covers and risk all of their lives. They just hoped that she felt the gravity of that.

Sarah wished there was something she could do to comfort Jenna—to renew her self-confidence. But that would most likely draw unwanted attention from Juan. Jake and Janie came into the breakfast room to join the women. Mendoza's men stood guard in the hallway.

Jake had just finished paying for their latest round of purchases and Juan carried their bags back to the limo. Janie was grateful that she wasn't wearing four inch heels like Sarah and Jenna were; she could tell that Sarah was beginning to regret that decision a bit too. She was a little too eager to sit down for lunch. Lunch was light and enjoyable despite the mounting tensions. Go time was rapidly approaching. Sarah watched for Jake to give the signal and squeezed Jenna's hand. They had picked this café because it allowed the limo to be conveniently parked in the alleyway. They had paid their bill and were leaving the café for the limo. Juan was helping Jenna, which left Jake and Janie in perfect position behind Mendoza's men. As they entered the alley, Juan noticed that the limo driver was missing.

Suddenly, two armed men came out of nowhere, shooting two of Mendoza's point men. Juan saw one of the men take aim at Sarah. He immediately turned and blocked her with his own body, taking a round of bullets to his back and shoulders. Janie was grazed in the thigh by a stray bullet.

It all happened in a matter of seconds. As Juan got up, Jake was there helping get Sarah to safety. Janie was leaning over Jenna. They all paused a beat to notice the carnage around them. Janie told Juan that Jenna was dead, as were the first two point men.

"We need to get out of here now," Jake shouted at them. "The cops will be showing up any minute." Juan agreed and Jake helped him into the limo. He stopped only for a moment to cross himself on behalf of his fallen comrades. They left the scene and made their way back to the hotel.

"Juan, we need to get you to a hospital, and then get the hell out of Paris. Hopefully they will think that this was just another terrorist attack. Janie, page the hotel concierge doctor."

"If you can hold my arm, I will change clothes and make sure that this doesn't come back to us," Juan said as he winced in pain. They all agreed. Only ten minutes had passed before the doctor came in. He told Sarah and Janie that he would need to rest, but that he was okay to fly. He removed the bullets and stitched Juan up.

"The police have already arrived at the scene," Jake announced. They found the limo driver bound and gagged in a nearby dumpster. The plane will be ready in three hours, I think we should all get cleaned up and rest a little before takeoff. Juan, you should probably call Mendoza and break the news about Jenna."

"Not necessary. My orders were only to protect Senora Sarah at all cost." Janie called room service to help them gather Jenna's things. Juan told them just to get rid of any evidence of the woman. BJ took the belongings and returned to the scene of the shooting. He told Jenna that everything had gone according to plan and that she was a free woman. He handed her the belongings and wished her the best with her new life.

Once they had landed safely back in New York, Jake called Reese to let him know what had happened. He assured him that Sarah was safe, but Jenna didn't make it. Jake let him know that Juan was on the other line with Mendoza. Sarah listened in on Juan's conversation with Mendoza and was disgusted with both of them for their complete disregard for human life. She did have to smile to herself though when she heard Juan tell Mendoza that he suspected the men were Absame's. The seed had been planted. Their plan couldn't be going any more smoothly.

Chapter Thirty-Five

Kat and Jako were all smiles. The first phase of the mission had been a perfect success. Ryan was in Washington smoothing over some French feathers that had been ruffled. Mendoza's men, as well as Absame's, were on their way to Cuba. Reese checked in and told Jako that everything was ready to go.

"See you after, and Reese…"

"Yes sir?"

"Make it by the book."

"Yes, sir."

"Alright everyone, let's go to work." Jako and Kat loaded their weapons and climbed in their SUV. With half the team missing, it was all hands on deck for this half of the mission.

Reese and his men were already waiting by the truck when Mendoza approached. Absame wasn't there yet, but it was still early. Reese was calm and collected, but Mendoza seemed more than a little on edge. When Absame finally arrived, he and Mendoza began inspecting the contents of the truck. They went through every case and examined every cartridge of ammo. Absame signaled for his men to bring the money. As Reese counted the cash,

Kat noticed four armed men coming out from behind a building. She didn't stop to think. She got out of the van and silently went up behind the men, knocking two of them out and slitting the third's throat. Before the fourth man could fire on her, Jako took him out. They loaded he men into the van just as Absame's men started looking around.

Reese had finished with the money and handed Mendoza the keys to the truck.

"I will see you later my friend."

"It's been a pleasure doing business with you as always," Reese replied. When Reese and the boys made it back to the hotel, Ryan was waiting in their suite dressed as a room service waiter.

"Well done men. When this is all over, make sure that you remember to thank Kat for your lives. Absame had a little surprise for you."

"I'll be sure to buy her a 'thank you' drink," Reese joked. The other two men agreed.

"Again, excellent work today. Both teams are safe and Jenna is a free woman. That's one hell of an accomplishment," Ryan told them.

"All in a day's work."

"I'll see everyone back at the compound."

Reese joined Mendoza for a drink in the bar. They would ride to the airport together.

"I am so very sorry about Jenna."

"Thank you, my friend. But I am very glad that Juan was able to keep your Sarah protected." The man had become totally obsessed with her, and Reese recognized that. Once reunited with Sarah, they joined Mendoza for dinner at Peter Luger Steak House. Dinner was a quiet affair for the most part. It seemed that the only one celebrating was Mendoza. He couldn't keep his eyes off Sarah and could barely stop himself from salivating. He had completely shrugged off Jenna's 'death' as if she had been a mere pet goldfish.

"That gown is very beautiful," he complimented Sarah. "Is it new?"

"It is. Jenna actually helped me pick it out before she was so tragically gunned down. I wear it now in her memory." The table grew tense for a moment. "To Jenna," Sarah said raising her glass. "To her being in a better place."

Meanwhile, Shawn and Thomas had followed Absame and his men to a port where they were loading a barge with several trucks. They couldn't get too close, but Thomas was able to make out the name on the barge. It looked like they had just come face to face with their next mission.

Absame left the port and made his way back to his Brownstone. Shawn stayed to watch the house while Thomas went to report their findings to Ryan and Jako.

"Well…this changes things a bit now doesn't it," Jako said. "Let me guess, no ATF?" Ryan just smiled. "I'll go get the information on the Dalles. Good job Tom."

"Thank you sir."

"You stay on Absame. Send Shawn to trail Mendoza. Jako, get the rest of the team to the compound ASAP," Ryan ordered.

"Yes sir," Thomas and Jako said in unison. Then, Ryan turned to Kat.

"You think you're ready for full service?"

Grinning from ear-to-ear, she gave an enthusiastic, "Hell yes!"

"Great. Excellent job today agent."

"Thank you sir," she said, still beaming.

Chapter Thirty-Six

Kat was so glad to be home; that's what the compound had become to her…home. She couldn't wait to begin training with the team. She settled into bad and popped the two pain pills and Ambien with a shot of Patron. She knew that this was not a good habit she was getting herself into, but she told herself that right now it was necessary to make sure that she got the sleep she needed to be her best.

Ryan arrived before daylight. He went to his rooms to put away his things. As he headed back downstairs, he ran into Sarah and Janie.

"Good morning ladies. I must say, you are both looking alive and well today. Glad to see it." They laughed at his silly humor.

"It's good to be alive, Ryan."

Kat and Reese had just sat down at the breakfast table; Bill and Jake weren't far behind. After the wait staff had delivered their plates and left the room, Ryan told the group that he was able to retrieve the barge's manifest.

"It is scheduled to set sail in a week because it is waiting on the late arrival of some cargo. They should be sailing right by us in approximately a week and a half. I know that doesn't give us much time, but we have to strike or let ATF in. This is the blow that will cripple Absame's organization, and Mendoza will feel it too. At the very least, it will put enough pressure on their partnership to collapse it. Reese, Sarah, Janie, Kat, and Jake, after your run and training, come to the command center to start running strategy. Bill and BJ, you will be responsible for preparing the weapons and other equipment."

After four hours of going through all the data they had gathered, they started to formulate a plan. Ryan came into command and told them to wrap it up for the day. He had just received word that Mendoza was back in town with a woman that he suspected was CIA.

"Do you think she is Radford's replacement?" Sarah asked.

"We haven't been able to confirm that yet. I'm hoping she's just undercover. However, the last time I spoke to her, she said she had just gotten a promotion, and that was right about the time that Radford had died. Jako and I have both worked with her in the past, so we are really going to need to stay in the shadows."

As if on cue, Reese's undercover line began ringing. "Reese, my friend, can you and your lovely wife join me and my new business acquaintance for dinner?" Mendoza asked. Ryan nodded his head, giving Reese the okay to accept the invitation.

"Of course. Just give me the place and time." Mendoza told him about a French restaurant that he'd been meaning to try.

"Be there by eight o'clock?"

"Great. See you then."

Back in New York, it was almost midnight as the last crate was loaded unto the Dalles. It was set to sail with the tide. Absame and his inner circle had just gotten out of the limo and were now headed up the gang plank. Absame went straight to his cabin to settle in for the journey. He didn't usually participate in this part of the deal, but this exchange was much too important not to.

The last thing to be loaded was the tobacco boat. There were two armed guards posted at each end of the boat. No one was allowed anywhere near it. Absame had already received partial payment on the secret item placed within the cabin of the tobacco boat. That partial payment in itself was more than what the rest of the shipment would bring in. After this deal, he could sever his ties with Mendoza and the brash American. Absame wasn't sure why he hated the man so much; he had done business with several Americans before. There was just something about this one that got under his skin. After this, he would never have to deal with anymore partners. He would just go home and live like a king for the rest of his life. His was getting too old for all of this.

A knock came at the cabin door. A sailor informed him that they were prepared to leave port. Absame would stay with the ship until they were off the coast of Mobile, Alabama in about a week. At that time, his crew would lower the tobacco boat into the water, and meet the buyer is Pensacola, Florida. There were always a lot of private boats, so they wouldn't draw attention to themselves. Once he was done, he would be able to disappear a much richer man.

His thoughts went to Kaitlyn for a moment. He still hadn't been able to find out anything about her. His new CIA informant had yet to prove herself as useful.

Reese, Sarah, Janie, and Jake pulled up in front of Galatoires Restaurant on Bourbon Street. The valet approached to help everyone out and park the limo. When they entered, Mendoza stood and kissed Sarah's hand, followed by Janie's. The mysterious new business acquaintance left the room almost as soon as they entered—no introductions had been made. Kat and Jako were ready to follow. Ryan had predicted that she wouldn't stay.

Mendoza asked Sarah if she would like him to order for her. He even invited Jake, Janie, and Juan to sit down with them.

"I thought your lady friend would be joining us as well," Reese asked.

"She had last minute business to attend to. You will meet her at the gala. Especially now that the lovely Sarah has some nice new gowns," Mendoza oozed. They were saved from further conversation when dinner was served.

Kat and Jako followed Mendoza's informant east on Bourbon Street. They almost thought she was going to leave the quarter, but instead she entered a private courtyard. They concealed themselves outside and watched as the light on the top floor went on. The woman came out onto the patio and looked out over the city. Ryan told them to make sure they got the address, but gave them the okay to head back. At the hotel, Ryan and Jako opted for room service while Kat went down to the bar.

Meanwhile, the group with Mendoza was just finishing their meal. He asked Reese to join him at this club for drinks. Reese had started to decline, when he heard Ryan in his ear telling him to go.

"Janie, please take Sarah home. Jake, you'll stay with me." Reese walked the women out as they waited for the limo to be brought up. Reese kissed Sarah on the cheek, "Don't wait up my love."

"Of course darling." Arriving back at the hotel, Sarah and Janie ran into Jako. "Hey, How'd it go tonight? Where's Kat?"

"She's still down at the bar. Been down there awhile actually," Jako told them. "I just checked on her though; she's alright." Janie and Sarah looked at each other then went to Janie's room.

"Are you worried about Kat?" Janie asked once they were inside.

"A little. I mean, after everything she's been through, it wouldn't be hard for the drugs to become a real problem. We're going to have to be really strong for her."

"She's such a strong and resilient person, but I agree. I think we should keep a closer eye on her."

Carly Hatch only had a few more days in New Orleans before she was due back in Quantico. If her superiors discovered what she had become a part of, she would end up dead or locked away at Leavenworth. So far, she hadn't found any connection between Ryan and Radford. Whoever this group was that was causing so much trouble for Mendoza and Absame, she was sure that they weren't with the American government. Carly hated becoming a traitor, but Absame had left her with little choice.

Finally, back at the compound, the group started with a solid run. Kat was feeling a little hungover from the night before, but she still managed to keep pace with Janie and Sarah. At about six miles, they stopped to stretch and get some water. Kat was fighting a losing battle within herself about whether or not to take the pills she had brought along in her backpack.

"If you're in pain, honey, take one," Janie said, seemingly reading her mind. Kat hesitated, but only for a second.

"Do you want to walk the rest of the way?" Sarah asked.

"No, I can finish," Kat insisted. She took off, but at a slower pace. Jake and the other were already showered and waiting by the time the women made it back to the compound.

Chapter Thirty-Seven

The next few days consisted of the team just enjoying the simple routine of life at the compound. They had been under a lot of pressure lately and were happy to just enjoy the luxuries that had been afforded to them.

It was the day of Mendoza's gala and Kat, Thomas, Shawn, and Jako were assigned to surveillance in the van. BJ would be outside with the limo. Jake and Janie were in their best professional evening attire. They would continue to play the role of trusty bodyguards to Reese and Sarah. When the pulled up in front of Mendoza's home, he was already waiting at the door with Absame and the woman from the other night. This time, Mendoza introduced her as Lisa.

"Her real name is Carly Hatch," Ryan said into their earpieces. Sarah was ready to leave the party before they even made it to the front door. It just made her sick to realize how easily a good cop could turn dirty. Was serving your country not sacred to anyone anymore? During dinner, she was seated between Mendoza and Carly, which she thought was odd. Reese was seated a few chairs down at the other side of the table. Carly attempted making conversation with Sarah, but Sarah could tell that she was just fishing for information so that she could determine if Sarah was who she said she was. *Oh come on honey, you can do better than that*, Sarah mused.

Throughout dinner, Mendoza mentioned plans to obtain a larger shipment of guns, but Absame showed no interest. This was a red flag.

"I have a bad feeling about this outcome," Ryan said, more to himself than to anyone else. Kat reported that Absame had left the restaurant and was headed straight to a private air strip. "Alright team," he said, "Get back to the compound when you can. I am leaving for DC to keep an eye on Carly there. Be ready for anything; I think this is all going to come to a head sooner than we think. Oh and Kat, come to my office when you get back. I want to talk to you before I leave."

"Yes sir." Janie and Sarah just looked at each other.

"What's going on?" Jake asked the women quietly.

"She's still in some pain," Janie answered.

"Is there a bigger problem that I should know about?"

"No," Sarah and Janie answered together.

"You would tell me if there was, wouldn't you?"

"Of course, Jake. She's one of is now. We have her back."

After getting back to the compound, Kat went straight to Ryan's office. He was still sitting behind his desk reviewing some documents.

"Kat, do you honestly feel that you are up for this mission?" he asked, getting right to the point. "If you are still in that much pain, you can stay in command and work the mission from there."

"No sir, I can do this."

"There is no shame in admitting when enough is too much."

"I know that sir, but it's not too much. I'm ready for this."

"Alright, well get some sleep because things are going to start moving a lot faster around here."

"Yes sir," she replied and left the room. Making it back to her room, she suddenly didn't feel as confident as she led Ryan to believe. But, she just knew that she wouldn't be able to live with herself if she stayed behind. She went to her drawer and took her medication—with water instead of liquor this time. *He's mine. I have to get him*, she thought as she drifted to sleep.

The next morning, the group went for a run. Kat made it all the way through without stopping and without needing any pain pills. But, the adrenaline of the run soon wore off and as soon as she made it back to her room, she began to feels the aches and pains creeping into her bones. She took her last couple of pills, then went downstairs to request a refill from the doctor. He talked to her about managing her pain and told her to take it easy the rest of the day. On her way back to her rooms, she asked Jako to just send a lunch tray up for her.

When she didn't come down for dinner either, the team was beginning to get concerned. Janie went up to check on her. She knocked, but there was no answer. Janie tried to knock one more time, and this time, Kat made her way to the door.

"Hey Janie. What's up?"

"Just checking on you. Everyone was worried when we didn't see you at dinner."

"No need. I'm just tired. The last couple of days have been pretty strenuous."

"Can I come in?"

"Sure. Can I get you something to drink?"

"No thank you."

"What's on your mind Janie?"

"Kat, are your pills becoming a problem for you?"

"Not at all. The fact that I'm still in pain and having trouble sleeping is becoming a problem for me."

"We're your family now—no matter what. We will walk through all kinds of things together. Even the strongest warrior needs a little help sometimes."

"Thanks Janie, I'll keep that in mind. Please tell the others that I'm fine." Janie gave her an understanding smile and placed a gentle hand on her shoulder before leaving. Kat closed the door and went back to her mini bar to pour another shot of Patron. She crawled into bed and popped a small cluster of pills, refusing to believe that she had a problem. *One of the world's deadliest terrorists couldn't kill me*, she thought as she drifted into sleep. *I'm not afraid of a few little pain pills.*

Chapter Thirty-Eight

In DC, Ryan was on his way to meet with Vice President Woods. Aaron answered the knock and motioned Ryan inside. The two met sat down and got right to business.

"Your hunch was right about Carly; she wasn't on assignment. She took personal leave," Woods told him. "She's also pulled all of the remaining files on Kat and tried to retrieve Carl's records. Look Ryan, I know you have a history with her. Do I need to bring someone else in?"

"No sir. I will handle it."

"For what it's worth…I'm sorry."

"It happens, sir. I just thought she was one of the good guys, that's all."

"How's the team doing? Are they ready for his next phase of the mission?"

"They are flawless sir, and I believe they are more than ready."

"Glad to hear it. Be safe out there Ryan— stay smart. I'll check in again before the mission."

"Yes sir." Ryan left the office and checked with the agent who had been tailing Carly. He told Ryan that she was at the Capital Grill with another CIA operative. Ryan knew that he had to play this carefully. Carly knew him very well. Ryan walked into the restaurant and went straight for the bar. Ryan ordered a Crown on the rocks and a T-bone steak, medium rare, with a baked potato and side salad. He hadn't looked around at all, but he could feel her eyes on the back of his neck. Ryan was halfway through his salad when the bartender brought him another drink.

"I didn't order this."

"It's from the lady across the room." Ryan turned around and hoped the artificial look on his face reflected both surprise and happiness to see her. It must have because she excused herself from her dinner companions and walked over to the bar. Kissing him on the cheek, Carly sat down next to him.

"I stopped by your place a few times," she said.

"I know, my doorway told me."

"Are you avoiding me?"

"Not at all, just been traveling a lot. You know how the secret service is; there's always some kind of emergency."

"Yes, I certainly haven't forgotten that."

"So how's the new job going?" he asked in between bites of his steak.

"Pretty boring actually. You know I've never been one for paperwork."

"I hear that," Ryan laughed. The bartender cleared his plates and Ryan ordered them another round of drinks.

"I miss the old days. Remember being fresh out of the academy; we were going to change the world."

"I still feel that way, don't you?"

"You want to get out of here?" She asked, changing the subject. "My new place is just around the corner." He knew he should say no, but he didn't want to make her suspicious. Ryan secretly hoped that what he told Woods about being able to handle this was true. Maybe he should have let the Vice President bring someone else in.

There was very little conversation as they made the drive back to her apartment. Talking was never their thing. They were so in tune with each other's body language, that they didn't notice the men following them. Once Carly and Ryan were inside the building, the men made a call to Absame to report what they had seen.

"Detain him immediately. I want to know who he is," Absame ordered.

Ryan woke before sunrise and gathered his belongings. There were roses by the door, so he took one and placed it on the pillow beside her. This would be the last time they would be together, and he knew it. It had to be.

One of Absame's men followed Ryan, while the other two went to retrieve Carly. She awoke to a knock at the door. She saw the rose on the pillow and got up. She opened the door expecting to see Ryan, but instead everything went black. When she regained consciousness, she didn't know where she was. She was tied securely to a chair in what looked like the cabin of a ship. The door opened and Absame entered. Carly felt the color drain from her face as she looked into his cold eyes. Absame struck her across the face so hard that the chair she was tied to tipped and hit the floor.

"Why have you not found anything for me? It's been weeks."

"I'm close to a breakthrough." Absame hit her again.

"Who was that man you were with?"

"He's just a friend, I swear it." Absame hit her again. She yelped in pain. "His name is Ryan. We have dated on and off for years. We went to the academy together."

"So he's CIA?"

"No, he pushed paper for homeland security." Absame contemplated her answer for a moment. Turning around, he picked up a long dagger from the table next to him.

"How you answer this next question is a matter of life and death." Carly couldn't take her eyes off the knife. "Were you able to get any information from this *Ryan*?"

"No, I..." was all Carly could manage before Absame severed her throat so severely that it almost removed her head. He turned to his men and instructed them to get rid of the body.

Ryan was on his way back to his own apartment and still hadn't noticed the man following him. He pushed the button to the elevator door and was hit from behind. The man that hit him, joined him on the ground only seconds later. Agent Riggs helped Ryan to his feet.

"Thank you."

"Sorry sir, I wasn't quite close enough to prevent the attack."

"What were you still doing there?"

"Just following orders, sir, from the Vice President, sir."

"Is Carly still being watched?"

"No sir, you signaled for us to leave."

"But you didn't?"

"No sir, orders." Ryan suddenly had a sick feeling in the pit of his stomach. He told Riggs to detain this man and then meet him back at Carly's apartment. Ryan tried calling her, but there was no answer. He parked out front and ran passed the doorway. The front door to her home stood wide open. Ryan pulled his weapon, but he already knew he was too late. Riggs was right behind him. They cleared the rooms. There were definite signs of a struggle. Ryan got on the phone with the Vice President, Jako, and Carly's superiors. Ryan told them the whole story. Carly's superior, Agent Cord, said that his team would take care of things from here. Ryan went home to get himself cleaned up. Just a few minutes later, his phone began to ring. It was Agent Cord requesting his presence at the morgue. Cord stopped him at the door.

"I know you two had history. I just feel like I need to prepare you for what you are about to see."

"I need to see her," Ryan pleaded. He immediately regretted going in there. It was truly the most horrific thing he had ever scene. He rushed out of the room; he thought he was going to throw up. What had she done to deserve this? Ryan made arrangements for an Agency funeral.

Chapter Thirty-Nine

At the compound, Jako had filled the team in on what was going on in DC, and that Ryan would be staying in the background for the remainder of the mission.

"For the next two days, we will be running mock exercises. There is an island approximately ten miles out. I have a freighter exactly like the one that Absame is on. Same amount of men on board. They don't know when they will be attacked, so it should be a fairly authentic simulation. Run the drill as many times as possible. Kat, you will be on Jake's team. Let's get busy."

They practiced their mock maneuvers all day. It would be time to head up for dinner soon. Then, they would head out to do the trial run on the ship. Jako had been observing all day. They were the tightest team he had ever seen. They opted to break into two teams: one on board the ship, and the other to cover the side boats. Janie was steering the boat for Jake's team. Kat was on point, and Thomas was in the middle with Jake. With the next team, BJ would sit as snipper to cover Sarah and Reese as they boarded the ship from the starboard side. Shawn and Bill were strategically placed on either side of the freighter to move in as back up and to detain any pirates that attempt to make a run for it. When it was time to cast off, Jako wished them all luck.

It took about an hour for them to arrive at the anchored ship. They split up and went in silent. The entire operation went down without a hitch in fifteen minutes. By the third run, they were able to shave off two minutes. Reese called it a night and they returned to the compound. Jako congratulated them on a job well done and told them to get a much deserved night of rest. Janie found Kat in the study and could tell how uncomfortable she was.

"Are you in pain?"

"Yes, but I don't want these stupid pills to own me."

"How about this…I'll hang onto your pills. That way, when you really need them, you can ask me and you won't be tempted to take them when you don't need them."

"Thank you Janie. Thank you so much." Janie handed her two pills and bid her goodnight.

Mendoza had just gotten off the phone with Absame. The anger surged through him. Absame was causing so much more trouble than they needed. It was one thing to kidnap an undercover CIA agent, but to kill one so brutally after her predecessor had shown up dead was reckless. Mendoza knew that he needed to rid himself of this barbaric man…and soon. The deal that was currently in motion would be their last. He trusted Reese much more, but in truth, he trusted no one.

Ryan was sitting in his DC office, finishing up some paperwork, when Cord came in.

"Have you found out anything on Carly's murder?"

"No actually. That's why I'm here. She took a leave of absence saying that her mother was ill in California, but her mother has been dead for over ten years. The hotel she booked said that she never checked in."

"What can I do to help?"

"Did she say anything to you that may have sent up a red flag?"

"No. We didn't really do a lot of talking when we saw each other." Ryan put his head in his hands for a moment. "I'm sorry, that was uncalled for."

"It's okay. I brought you the last few files for some of her more recent cases. For your eyes only."

"Thank you Cord." Cord had a feeling that Ryan wasn't being level with him, but that was just the nature of their line of work. A little while later the two men left for Carly's private service. There was only one other person present, which broke his heart. As they laid her to rest in the cemetery, Ryan noticed to figures standing in the tree line. They had been following him all day. He was sick and tired of this cat and mouse game. He should be back at the compound with his team.

When Ryan got back to his apartment, he swept the entire place for bugs. He found three, so he went into the bathroom and turned on the shower and called Jako with an update.

Reese, Sarah, Jake, and Janie decided to spend the day in New Orleans. That way, Mendoza would have no reason to suspect anything. Kat was beginning to feel the effects of withdrawal since Janie had begun monitoring her consumption. Janie had only left her enough to get her by while they were away. She took them all at once, but didn't get any relief. She paced back and forth in her room before deciding to go for a run. That didn't seem to help much either, so she went down to see the doctor. He gave her an injection and refilled her prescription. He told her to come back if she didn't get better and he would give her something else. The shot helped almost immediately. She went back upstairs to enjoy the sweet feeling of relief.

Chapter Forty

It was time. They did last minute checks on all of their procedures and equipment and gathered at the bottom of the stairs. They left for the docks shortly thereafter. Jako stood overlooking the balcony, watching them leave. He hated this part of their missions. He went back to command to make sure that everything was ready and working properly.

Janie had picked the ship up on radar. In five hundred feet, they would cut the engines. Fifty feet out, both teams got in the water and swan silently into position. As soon as they got the green light from Vice President Woods, their snipper took out the guards on watch. Both teams moved swiftly and in unison to take over the ship just as they had practiced in their mock drills. They had gained control of the vessel in ten minutes flat. The only thing they hadn't counted on was Absame being nowhere to be found. Kat reached the wayward side of the ship. As she got close to the rail, her radioactive badge went off. At that same moment, she was attacked from behind. All that time practicing in the ring had served her well; it didn't take long for her to dispatch her attacker and radio for help. Janie announced that there was a small vessel on radar. Kat was livid; Absame had gotten away! Jake and Reese were the first to reach her.

Reese ordered Thomas to pursue the small boat; the rest went back to their ship to secure the location.

From out of nowhere, a shot rang out. Sarah and Thomas were hit. BJ located the shooter and took him out in seconds, then took off after the boat with Shawn and Bill close behind. Kat ran over to Sarah, and Jake went to assist Thomas. They field dressed the wounds and gave each a shot of morphine. Sarah had just been grazed by the bullet, but Thomas had taken the shot dangerously close to his heart. During all of the commotion, Kat had given herself an injection of morphine. She quickly looked around to make sure that no one saw anything. She would come up with an excuse for the missing syringe later. Right now, they had work to do.

They made a thorough sweep of the ship. Reese found a map that had been half burned. He put it in his pocket and concluded their search. Upon returning to the compound, they rushed to the main house and down to the hospital ward with Sarah and Thomas. Jako was waiting for them there. Reese rushed down a few minutes later and asked how they were doing.

"Sarah is being stitched up now and should be out in just a few minutes. She'll be a little sore for a few days, but she's gonna be fine. Thomas has a long road ahead of him. His heart is under a lot of stress." Just then, the doctor came out.

"We did all we could do. The damage was too severe to the tissue around the heart. I'm so sorry, but we couldn't save him."

Jako led everyone up to command where the Vice President and Ryan were waiting on the intercom. The group was very solemn as they made their way upstairs. After the debriefing, Vice President Woods told them not to be discouraged.

"The only way to honor Thomas is to catch that son-of-a-bitch Absame and make him pay for everything he has put you all through."

They left command and gathered in the study. Kat grabbed a bottle of Irish Whiskey that she knew was Thomas' favorite. She poured them each two fingers and they toasted to his life. Reese excused himself first so that he could check on Sarah before calling it a night. She was resting peacefully. He sat beside her for a moment, just holding her hand. The rest of the team turned in for the evening; everyone was exhausted.

Mendoza had just received word that their ship had not made it to the check point. He was trying feverishly to get ahold of Absame, but wasn't having much luck. He tried calling Reese next.

"I'm sorry to wake you, my friend. Can you meet me for brunch on Bourbon Street at eleven o'clock?"

"Of course. Is everything okay?"

"Not on the phone."

"See you tomorrow." Reese got Janie and Jake up and told them that they needed to get to New Orleans right away in case Mendoza changed his mind. He was worried that Sarah wouldn't be up for the trip, but she insisted that she was fine and ready to go. They had made the right call because Mendoza was at their door at sunrise.

"I'm sorry to disturb you so early, but this can't wait. I need to talk to you now."

"What's going on?" Reese asked.

"We lost the shipment. I can't find Absame."

"Look, Mendoza, I'm sorry, but I just don't see how I can help."

"I need to replace that order…and fast. The people I sold to don't handle complications like this very well."

"It would take me a few days to duplicate a shipment of that size."

"Thank you, my friend. I knew I could count on you. It wouldn't surprise me if that bastard Absame took the shipment. We need to find him."

"Calm down. Let me make some calls. I will get back to you this afternoon."

BJ, Shawn, and Bill had been able to keep up with Absame while remaining off the radar. Absame had gone to shore for fuel and supplies. It looked as if something was about to happen. BJ called Jako.

"Sir, I swam in as close as I could. You need to get the team here before sunrise. If I translated right, they have a buyer for the item that Absame had hidden in the tobacco boat. It's a bomb, sir—a big one."

Jako reported to Ryan, who immediately got the Vice President involved. Then, he got on the phone with Reese and told him that they needed to get back immediately.

"I'll fill you in when you get here."

Chapter Forty-One

Everyone made their way into command. "Thanks for the hustle team," Ryan began over the intercom. "From the satellite images we were able to collect from Absame's position, he definitely has a hot bomb. You need to get there as soon as possible before this exchange goes down. If we don't strike fast, there is going to be a massive loss of life on American soil."

They suited up and headed out. They would try to get as close to Absame's location as they could. They were going to utilize their scuba gear for this attack. With the sniper rifles locked and loaded, they should be able to make this problem go away in a matter of seconds. Ryan requested that Absame be taken alive, but he certainly wouldn't blame anyone for giving the man what he deserved. He probably wouldn't talk even if they were successful in capturing him. BJ, Shawn, and Bill were relieved to see the rest of the team show up. They hit the water and BJ gave them fifteen minutes before he moved the boat in a little closer. He prepared his sniper rifle and got ready to get this party started. Once the green light sounded in their ears, BJ squeezed the trigger and took out the two sentry guards—almost without a sound. Sarah and Reese boarded the boat while the others rushed the shoreline.

Kat and Jake went straight to the house. Reese and Sarah joined Janie in rounding up Absame's men on shore once the boat had been cleared. Jake was in hand-to-hand combat with Ayiid and two others. Kat went in search of Absame. She found him passed out between two women. Kat quietly woke the women and sent them out of the room. She then pushed Absame over the side of the bed.

"Wake up asshole. I want you to see the person that's about to end your life." Absame looked confused. Kat laughed. "You don't even recognize my voice? Aww, Absame that hurts kind of."

"Kaitlyn?" He asked as terror and recognition filled his eyes simultaneously. Then, both of those were replaced with anger. He kicked her away and got to his feet. He hit her three times across the face—hard. She fell backwards, but he picked her up and was about to hit her again, when she sunk her knife into his chest. Jake came in just as Absame was sliding to the floor. Kat just stood there trembling. Jake rushed to her side and folded her in his arms.

"Shhhh, it's okay. It's over. It's over. He can't hurt you anymore."

Ryan was relieved to hear his entire team call, "Clear" into his ear. Then, he received the report of Absame's death. Janie reported that the bomb had been secured.

"Excellent. A containment team will be there soon," Ryan informed. "A helicopter is on its way to bring you home."

Kat snuck away to give herself a morphine shot. Each person's pack was equipped with one, and it would be a while before hers was missed. If anything, she would just say that it was lost in her struggle. She hated lying to the team, but what she hated even more was how good she was becoming at it. Once they had settled onto their flight, Kat began pretending to rummage through her backpack.

"Is something wrong Kat?" Janie asked.

"I'm in a lot of pain from the struggle with Absame. I was just looking for my hypo, but it must have fallen out." Janie and Sarah exchanged looks. Jake reached into his bag and handed her his needle. After the second shot, she was feeling much calmer. Jake asked if she were feeling any better and she nodded her head 'yes' and closed her eyes. She adjusted in her seat to get more comfortable for a nap, when she suddenly yelped in pain. Sarah jumped up and helped her sit back. She was trying to get her vest undone. Reese used his knife to cut it away. There was a gaping hole below her left shoulder. Sarah took out her syringe and gave Kat another dose. Janie pulled out her first aid kit and cleaned the wound. A bullet had gone straight through Kat's vest. Kat hadn't even realized that she had been shot. Reese got on the phone and requested that a medical team be standing by when they arrived. Jake and Reese helped Kat lay down on the floor so that Sarah could hold a tight compress to her shoulder. Janie had started a field IV. When they arrived at the compound, the doctor replaced the IV with a morphine drip.

"Go get cleaned up everyone. I will stay with her," Jako told the group. The doctor came out an hour later and told Jako that the surgery had gone better than expected. Kat was now resting peacefully in recovery. Jake, Sarah, and Janie took terms sitting with her throughout the night. *This feels familiar*, Jake thought to himself as he watched her sleep.

Chapter Forty-Two

Mendoza received a call from his buyer and they were not happy. They wanted to know what he was going to do about Absame's death and the missing bomb they had already put ten million dollars down on. Mendoza felt as though he had been punched in the gut.

"I don't know anything about a bomb. What I sold you was guns and ammo."

"Mendoza you need to make this right. You have one week and not a second more. If you don't deliver, your death won't even compare to Absame's."

"I understand."

"I suggest you do more than that within the next seven days, or you will suffer the consequences of failure." Then, the line went dead. Mendoza's angry yells echoed throughout Bourbon Street. He beat two of his guards to a pulp and ordered Juan to bring him a whore. The woman's screams were horrific, but seemed to be muffled. When Mendoza emerged from the room, he was covered in her blood. He told Juan to dump her body in the swamps. Juan brought two men into the room to help. Everything was covered in blood and there wasn't much left to the woman's body. One of the men ran from the room, crossing himself against evil. Juan and the other men heard a gunshot and found his body crumpled on the floor when they made their way downstairs.

"Anyone else have a problem?" Mendoza shouted. Not a word was spoken.

Reese's undercover line rang just as they were finishing dinner.

"Whoa, Mendoza, wait…slow down. I can't understand a word you're saying." Reese put the phone on speaker.

"My friend, Absame is dead. He had to be the one stealing our shipments. He took money from ISIS and now there is a bomb that is missing."

"A bomb!"

"I knew nothing about the deal. I thought we were just selling guns and ammo, but now they are holding me responsible. They are giving me a week to either deliver the bomb or the ten million dollars they paid Absame for it. Please, Reese, you have to help me."

"I can make some calls. Give me a day or two. Lay low Mendoza."

"Thank you, my friend. I will be able to rest easier now." Reese ended the call and Ryan told them to meet him in command in an hour.

"I think our best course of action is to use the bomb as bait," Ryan suggested. "That way, we nail Mendoza and the new players."

"Make it happen," the Vice President authorized. "But let Mendoza sweat for another day or two."

"Yes sir." The team returned to their rooms for the evening. Kat went in her room and took her pain medication. At least she was actually in pain this time. She waited half an hour for the pills to kick in, then took three more and chased them with a double shot of Southern Comfort.

Sarah was having trouble sleeping as well, so she went down to the study to have a drink and sit with a book for a little while. Reese came in behind her. The sound of his voice made her jump.

"I knew I would find you here," he chuckled.

"And how did you know that?"

"Because you and I have quite a bit in common. This is one of them," he said sitting down across from her with a drink of his own. "So, Sarah, what's on your mind?"

"I'm actually a little bummed that the mission will be over soon. I don't know if I can go back to boring old life in London."

"You don't have to go back."

"There's nothing holding me here without the work." At that, Reese leaned in and kissed her.

"There is if you want there to be."

Chapter Forty-Three

Reese's phone had started to ring before they even finished breakfast. "Mendoza, it's only been seven hours. This is going to take a little time. I promise to do my best."

"Okay my friend. I will see you soon."

After breakfast, the team met briefly in command.

"Reese, I'm going to need you to get the specifics on the bomb. We don't want anyone getting suspicious at this point in the game," Ryan told him. Reese left for a moment to call Mendoza back. The techs would recrate the bomb so that it would be convincing, but useless.

The team went for their morning run, then spent some time at the shooting range. When Kat made it back to her room to shower, she just collapsed on the bed. She reached into her backpack and pulled out a syringe. She had taken some needles from the hospital; the pills just weren't working any more. She hated herself for lying to everyone, her family. She hated herself even more for not being able to control herself.

After lunch, they all met back in command to formulate plans for this final hoorah. After the meeting, Sarah and Janie asked if they could have a word privately with Ryan and Jako. The four of them went into the study and closed the door.

"Is this about Kat?"

"Yes, you can see it too."

"Of course. We are just hoping that she can keep it together through this mission, and then we have arrangements in place to help her detox. We are her family now and we are going to help her through this like a family." Sarah and Janie felt so much better after the conversation. They met up with everyone else upstairs.

Reese, Sarah, Jake and Janie would fly into New Orleans first thing in the morning. BJ, Shawn, Bill, and Kat would stay behind to help formulate the behind the scenes operations. Reese made contact with Mendoza as soon as they arrived at the townhouse. Mendoza was eager to ask questions, but Reese convinced him to wait until they could talk in person. They planned to meet at the sidewalk café at noon.

Kat was in her room when she heard a knock at the door. She was surprised to see Ryan standing there. He handed her a package. She opened it and her heart sank when she saw that it was filled with drugs and needles. She started to say something, but he held up a hand to stop here.

"We are going to deal with this later. In the meantime, make sure that you can pull yourself together enough to not get your comrades killed in this mission." She tried to apologize, but he stopped her again. "I know Kat, it's not your fault. You've been through a hell of a lot. You have more support than you know. We helped you get through before, and we will be here to help you get through this too."

"Thank you sir," she couldn't stop the tears from rolling down her cheeks.

Reese and the others pulled into the restaurant just in time. The men took a table outside.

"I have a line on the product, but it's going to take a few days. There's going to be some out of pocket costs too. This product isn't cheap."

"Make the deal my friend. I will cover the difference."

"Very good. I will make the arrangements. I am flying out later today, but will be in touch."

"Thank you my friends." Mendoza went to kiss Sarah's hand, but she just walked out of the restaurant. He didn't seem offended.

They made it back to the compound just in time for dinner. The discussion was of their plans for the final mission. As the group talked, Kat looked around at all of the people who had become so special to her. She knew that, no matter what, she couldn't let them down. They spent the next several hours reviewing the data the techs had gathered so far. After another round of drinks, Jake and Kat decided to take a walk while the rest went up to bed. Reese walked Sarah to her door and surprised her with a kiss.

"You know that I'm not going to let that animal hurt you, don't you?" Reese asked, tucking a stray hair behind her ear.

"I know," she smiled. "Just being around him makes me sick to my stomach."

"It will all be over and done soon enough."

"Are you worried about the mission?" She asked.

"No, I'm not. I know it won't be easy, but we'll make it through. And, then I would like to take you on a real date."

Jake and Kat walked around the entire grounds. When they made it to a secluded part of the gardens, he took her in his arms and kissed her.

"I hope you know that I'm not going to let you go," he told her.

"I'm not going anywhere," she smiled. They walked back to the compound arm-in-arm. Jake walked her to her door and kissed her goodnight.

Chapter Forty-Four

The team sat in command reviewing new intel from the techs. They worked non-stop for hours. BJ, Shawn, and Bill had been able to hack into the ISIS group's security system, allowing them to receive a live feed.

"They have at least twenty men that we can confirm, but probably more," Ryan told them. "Reese, how many men do you think Mendoza will have with him?"

"At least six."

"That leaves us way outnumbered," Jako said.

"We've been outnumbered before. We can do this," Jake said.

"Alright, Reese, call Mendoza and have him set up the meet with the buyer at the docks in Mobile at midnight—two nights from now. The rest of you, that gives us two days to become expert marksmen. I want all of you to become familiar with every single weapon in that arsenal and spend as many hours as you can at target practice."

"Yes sir!" They all said enthusiastically.

It was D-Day and the team was preparing to make their way down to the docks. They were more ready than they had ever been. Reese, Sarah, and Janie took the helicopter to accompany Mendoza to the docks. Jake, Kat, and BJ arrived two hours earlier to set up sniper cover. Shawn and Bill manned the surveillance tent to make sure they could get the team real-time intel when needed.

It was time. Jake cut the engines approximately two thousand feet out. They would swim the rest of the way. There were four men walking the perimeter; each team member silently took out a guard. They climbed up into position and signaled when they were ready. ISIS showed up with ten men instead of two, as Mendoza had requested.

"Eliminate as many as you can, as quietly as you can," Ryan whispered into their earpieces. Jake and Kat waited for them to line up in their positions, and then quietly slit four of their throats. The other four men were inside with the one that was believed to be their leader. Jake and Kat took their robes and stood in their assumed positions. Just then, the limo pulled up, Janie and one of Mendoza's men got out first. As soon as Reese, Sarah, and Mendoza entered the warehouse, all hell broke loose outside. Ten additional men swarmed the building. BJ, Kat, and Jake opened fire, while Juan and Janie engaged in some hand-to-hand combat. The battle only lasted mere seconds, but it felt so much longer. Jake looked around to take inventory of his team. It looked like they had come out the winners on this one. When they rushed into the building, all of the ISIS members were dead, Reese was shot on the floor, and Mendoza was holding a gun to Sarah's head.

"I'm going to walk out of here with the bomb, the money, and Sarah. If you want her alive, you're going to let me do that," Mendoza shouted.

"You have three rifles pointed right at you man. You really think we are going to let that happen?" Jake said. In the brief second it took Mendoza to hesitate, Sarah grabbed his gun and pushed it upwards. BJ took the shot, hitting Mendoza in the temple. Most of the team had been injured in some way. They helped each other to the safety of the helicopter and got the hell out of there.

Ryan and Jako were standing by with a medical team when then landed at the compound. Reese had to be carried in on a gurney, but the others were able to walk themselves down to the hospital ward. Jako slapped Ryan on the back when they realized that everyone was alive and accounted for. Not to mention that the mission had been a complete success.

"You know what, this country has one incredible insurance policy with this team," Jako said. Ryan laughed.

"You got that right! Looks like we are going to have to turn this into full-time employment for these guys." The men smiled to each other and followed the group downstairs. Reese was in surgery for two hours. It seemed like an eternity before the doctor came out and told everyone that he was going to be just fine. They gathered in the study a little while later to toast their lives and their success.

"Congratulations!" Ryan bellowed. "You truly are the best of the best." After another round. Everyone went to bed. Sarah grabbed a blanket and went down to sleep in the chair next to Reese's bed.

The next morning, Jako went around knocking on doors. He wanted everyone downstairs for breakfast in fifteen minutes. Then, he went downstairs to get Reese and Sarah. When they all entered the study, Ryan was standing there was Vice President Woods. There were several suitcases already packed and lining the wall.

"I believe sincere congratulations are in orders," Woods told the room of confused faces. "We have taken the liberty of packing your bags for you."

"Kicking us out already?" Jake asked.

"Yes, your plane leaves in an hour."

"Where are we going?"

"We thought two weeks' vacation in Hawaii was appropriate. Is that alright with you all?" A couple of jaws hit the floor while other just nodded, awestruck. "After two weeks of rest and relaxation, you will be taken to your new compound to receive your next orders."

"What? You mean…we're staying?"

"You are the best task force this country has ever seen. We would be stupid to let you go," Ryan answered. As the group celebrated, Ryan pulled Kat aside and told her that she would be in a detox facility for the next couple of weeks, and that he sincerely hoped she would rejoin the team afterward.

"Thank you so much sir…for everything. I would be honored to remain a part of this team."

The End

www.ingramcontent.com/pod-product-compliance
Lightning Source LLC
Chambersburg PA
CBHW030311200626
46816CB00002BA/849